I'd been avoiding Mother's calls for days.

She was anxious to finalize her plans for my elaborate wedding, and I'd hoped by putting her off that she would finally cease and desist.

Guilt prompted me to pick up the phone and face the consequences.

"Good morning, Mother. How are you?"

"I'm perfectly fine, but I was beginning to worry that you'd fallen off the face of the earth, Margaret. It's a relief to know you're alive and well." Mother cloaked her sarcasm in such a soft, sweet tone it took a few seconds to realize I'd been zinged.

"Business is booming."

"Not too booming for you to have lunch with your mother today, I hope?"

When she referred to herself in the third person, I knew I was in trouble, so I bit the bullet. "Of course not. Just the two of us?"

"There's someone at the door," Mother replied without responding to my question. "I'll see you at noon."

With a feeling of foreboding, I hung up the phone. I feared the wedding-planning trap had been sprung.

Charlotte Douglas

USA TODAY bestselling author Charlotte Douglas, a versatile writer who has produced over twenty-five books, including romance, suspense, Gothic, and even a *Star Trek* novel, has now created a mystery series featuring Maggie Skerritt, a witty and irreverent homicide detective in a small fictional town on Florida's central west coast.

Douglas's life has been as varied as her writings. Born in North Carolina and raised in Florida, she earned her degree in English from the University of North Carolina at Chapel Hill and attended graduate school at the University of South Florida in Tampa. She has worked as an actor, a journalist and a church musician and taught English and speech at the secondary and college level for almost two decades. For several summers while newly married and still in college, she even manned a U.S. Forest Service lookout in northwest Montana with her husband.

Married to her high school sweetheart for over four decades, Douglas now writes full-time. With her husband and their two cairn terriers, she divides her year between their home on Florida's central west coast—a place not unlike Pelican Bay—and their mountaintop retreat in the Great Smokies of North Carolina.

She enjoys hearing from readers, who can contact her at charlottedouglas1@juno.com.

CHARLOTTE DOUGLAS

Wedding Bell Blues

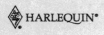

From the Author

Dear Reader,

Welcome back to Pelican Bay! This month Maggie is inundated by all things bridal.

She and Bill Malcolm are hired to find a runaway bride and to provide security for a wedding reception. At the same time, Maggie struggles to convince her mother and sister that she doesn't want them to plan for her "the biggest wedding Pelican Bay has ever seen." But all is not beribboned bouquets and white lace as Maggie and Bill's search for the missing bride-to-be turns into a full-blown murder investigation.

My mail has been filled with requests for Maggie and Bill to tie the knot. Will their marriage finally happen in *Wedding Bell Blues*? Or will commitment-shy Maggie balk again? Relax, smell the orange blossoms and enjoy Maggie's latest adventure.

Happy reading!

Charlotte Douglas

**Maggie Skerritt Mysteries
by Charlotte Douglas**

WEDDING BELL BLUES
SPRING BREAK
HOLIDAYS ARE MURDER
PELICAN BAY

"Good morning, Maggie—if you like this hot, sticky weather." Darcy Wilkins, my secretary-receptionist and jill-of-all-trades, dropped the mail on my desk.

"Like it or not," I said, "it'll be this way for the next six months. Thank God for air-conditioning."

Darcy handed me a jumbo French-vanilla latte from the bookstore coffee shop downstairs and settled on the sofa in my office. Cupping a mug of green tea in her capable dark hands, she propped her feet on the coffee table and waited for further instructions.

In the far corner of the sofa, Roger, the pug I'd inherited from a former client, slept undisturbed, his legs straight in the air in the dying cockroach position, head hanging backward over the cushion's edge. His snuffling snore mixed with the rumble of traffic on Main Street one storey below where the morning rush could be heard, even through closed windows and above the hum of central cooling.

I sorted through the stack of envelopes and set aside the utility bills for Darcy to handle. My morning started going downhill at the sight of an oversize white linen envelope addressed to Miss Margaret Skerritt, Pelican Bay Investigations, Pelican Bay, Florida. In the same elegant script, the return address indicated the plump package was from Mrs. Philip Skerritt, my mother.

Knowing what I'd find, I slit the envelope and dumped its contents on my desktop with a sigh.

"June is busting out all over," I said to Darcy, "and I'm running out of places to hide."

She arched an eyebrow in question. Roger snored louder.

"Hide?" Darcy said with a hint of disbelief. "I wouldn't think you, a tough ex-cop and Pelican Bay's finest female private eye, would hide from anything."

"I'm the city's *only* woman P.I.," I said, "and if you had my mother, you'd be looking for a bolt hole, too."

I indicated the pile of brochures and magazine and newspaper clippings heaped on my desk. "Everywhere I look are articles on planning weddings and ads for brides' dresses, florists, caterers, and honeymoon travel packages. The newspapers are filled with wedding announcements. And, to make certain that I don't miss something, Mother gathers them all up and sends them to me."

"But you're not getting married until Valentine's Day. That's more than eight months away."

"Right."

"And I thought you and Bill had agreed on a small wedding?"

"We have."

She pointed to the small mountain of materials on my desktop. "Then why the bridal blitz?"

Why, indeed? "Mother dear, who has ignored me my entire life, had a change of heart in April after she suffered what might have been a fatal stroke. Now she's determined to compensate for her former neglect by throwing me the biggest wedding Pelican Bay has ever seen." I shuddered. "And when she and Caroline put their heads together, you can bet they're planning an extravaganza to rival the distant nuptials of Charles and Diana. The only thing missing will be global television coverage."

Darcy shrugged. "Can't you just say no?"

"Mother's selectively deaf when she doesn't want to hear something."

"And your sister?"

"Caroline thinks I'm being coy. My sister can't believe there's a woman on earth who doesn't want a huge, elaborate wedding. It involves shopping, after all, Caroline's raison d'être."

"And what does Bill say?"

I shook my head. "He's no help. He says he'll go along with whatever I decide."

"And you've decided?"

I nodded. "No big wedding."

"Then there's no problem."

"Except breaking that news to my mother and sister, who refuse to accept the fact. They're pushing me now to sign up for bridal registries."

"That's not a bad idea."

"But we don't need anything. I have my furnished condo, and Bill's family home in Plant City is full of his parents' antique furniture and his mother's china, silver, and crystal."

"There must be something you want."

I thought for a second. "I could use a new sidearm."

"There you go," she said with a grin that exposed perfect white teeth. "Register at Cole's Gun Shop."

"And give my mother another stroke? I don't think so. I couldn't live with the guilt."

"Where's your groom-to-be today?"

"Helping the Pelican Bay Historical Society by running free background checks on their volunteers."

Darcy looked surprised. "They research their volunteers? Aren't most of them little old ladies?"

"The museum docents present several programs a year for children. The director figures he can't be too careful."

Darcy nodded, her expression solemn, and I guessed she was thinking what I was. Our last major case had involved a pedophile who had murdered three young girls in Tampa. Checking out anyone who worked with kids was no longer optional. It was a necessity.

Darcy drained the last of her tea and pushed to her feet. I handed her the bills to pay, and she went into the reception area and closed the door behind her.

I picked up the wastebasket and swept my arm across the top of my desk to file Mother's latest correspondence. I wished I could dispose of my reservations about my rapidly approaching marriage as easily.

Bill Malcolm, my fiancé and co-owner of Pelican Bay Investigations, had been my first partner when I'd joined the Tampa Police Department twenty-three years ago. He'd also been my best friend almost that long, even when I transferred to the Pelican Bay Department after seven years with Tampa. Last Christmas, he'd proposed. I loved him, without doubt, but whether I was marriage material remained to be seen. I'd led a schizophrenic life. Raised in privilege and wealth, I'd changed course at twenty-six to become a police officer when the love of my youth, an ER doctor, had been murdered by a crack addict. I'd dived headfirst from the height of society into the underworld of crime.

Earlier this year, after more than two decades as a police officer, I'd retired from the force. But as a private investigator, I still straddled both worlds, belonging in neither. Police work had been all-consuming, and I'd had no time for diversions, no hobbies and very few friendships, besides Bill. I'd grown solitary, withdrawn, and set in my ways. Somewhere along the way, I'd forgotten how to enjoy living. My first career had been as a librarian, yet over the years, I'd rarely taken the opportunity to read, which at one time had been one of my greatest pleasures.

Although I'd committed to marry Bill—we'd even closed last month on a house we had bought together—I feared I didn't have what it took to live the rest of my life with another human being, even one as wonderful as Bill.

Especially one as wonderful as Bill.

My biggest concern was that I would either drive him nuts or out of my life entirely.

I looked at Roger, still sleeping peacefully, if not quietly. I had committed to owning a dog and surprised myself by enjoying it. Maybe there was hope for me yet.

A knock sounded, and Darcy slipped into my office and closed the door behind her.

"You've got visitors."

"Clients?"

She hesitated. "I think so."

"You're not sure?"

"It's Wanda Weiland."

My heart stopped. "The wedding planner?"

She nodded and flashed an apologetic smile. "As in Weddings by Wanda."

My fight-or-flight response kicked in, raising my

pulse and respiration rate, as I considered the possibility that Wanda had been sent by my mother. An ambush on my own turf.

"She's not alone," Darcy added.

"Please tell me my mother's not with her." I gazed at the second-story window and contemplated a jump as my only means of escape.

Roger, now wide awake and on alert, watched me with an eager look, as if reading my thoughts. He flashed his full-focus grin and wagged his tail. If I jumped, Roger would follow. The crazy pooch was game for anything.

I considered my options. The fall probably wouldn't kill me, but I might break a leg, so I couldn't run. Unable to flee, I'd be completely at Mother's mercy. I abandoned the idea of a header onto Main Street and sucked up to face the music.

"The other woman isn't your mother," Darcy said. "She's younger than your mother, but older than you."

"Not Caroline?" I could probably get rid of the wedding planner, but I didn't want to be double-teamed by my persistent older sister.

Darcy shook her head. "I've met Caroline. It's not her, but whoever she is, she's too distraught to give her name."

Distress could be real or an act. I wouldn't put it past Mother and Caroline to stoop to a ploy to reel me in, but I could handle Wanda and a stranger, who'd be more reasonable than my family members. Everyone was more reasonable than my relatives. I told Darcy to show them in.

Darcy went to fetch them, and I called Roger and set him on my lap. He'd never met a leg he didn't love, and his humping could be bad for business, so when clients arrived, I kept him on a short leash.

Wanda Weiland breezed through the door, looking as fresh and blushing as a bride herself in a clingy floral dress, strappy sandals and makeup that gave her a perfect healthy glow. Her long auburn hair swung as she walked, and she flung it off her shoulders with a snap of her head and took a chair across from my desk. She looked to be in her late thirties or possibly even forties. These days it was hard to tell whether a woman had good genes or an excellent plastic surgeon.

In contrast, the woman with her looked like an emotional wreck. Although she was neatly dressed in tailored slacks, a silk blouse and pearls, her complexion was splotched from crying, her eyes red-rimmed. She clutched a damp Kleenex in one hand, her purse in the other. She stopped just inside the door and appeared dazed and disoriented. She didn't sit until Wanda patted the seat of the chair next to her.

"Thank you for seeing us on such short notice," Wanda said.

"It's an emergency," the other woman added with a shiver, her voice hoarse from tears. "My daughter's missing."

"I read about you in the newspapers," Wanda said, "how you solved Senator Branigan's murder. I told Jeanette you could help us."

"Jeanette?" I said.

"Jeanette Langston," the distraught woman introduced herself. "I hope you can help me. I don't know where else to turn."

"You've been to the police?" I asked.

Jeanette nodded. "I spoke with the sheriff's department. They told me there's been no sign of a crime, and since Alicia left messages assuring us that she's all right, they won't get involved."

I eyed Jeanette and estimated that she was older than me, somewhere in her mid-to-late fifties. Years ago, I would have assumed her daughter to be a grown-up, but with current advances in medical science and women having babies later in life, I took nothing for granted.

"Tell me about Alicia," I said.

"She's supposed to be married at the end of this month," Jeanette said with a hitch in her voice.

Unless something kinky was going on, that fact made Alicia an adult. And it also explained the presence of Wanda, the wedding planner.

"Here's her picture." Jeanette slid a four-by-six photo across my desk.

I picked it up and studied the pretty girl posed on a seawall, long blond hair flowing in the wind, hazel eyes smiling at the camera. Tall and slender, she had an air of seriousness lurking beneath the happiness on her face.

"Alicia's disappeared?" I said.

Jeanette nodded. "Four days ago. She left a note saying not to worry about her. And a voice mail a day later, assuring me that she's okay. But I've tried calling her cell phone and she doesn't answer. Garth, her fiancé, hasn't heard a word from her, either."

"So she's a runaway bride."

Even I, who never went to the movies and seldom turned on a television, was familiar with the Julia Roberts chick flick. I'd watched it late one night in the throes of insomnia and had felt a special kinship with the character who couldn't commit.

"She's not a runaway," Jeanette said with obvious conviction.

Wanda, so far, had nothing to add but a reassuring pat of Jeanette's hand.

"Not cold feet?" I said. "You're sure?"

Jeanette shook her head without ruffling a strand of her honey-colored dye job. "Alicia *loves* Garth. They've been engaged for three years. A year ago they began planning this wedding to take place when Alicia finished graduate school."

"Still," I said reasonably and with a strong degree of empathy for Alicia, "she could be having second thoughts."

"She did say in her note to cancel the wedding plans," Wanda interjected.

"Big wedding?" I asked.

Wanda nodded. "Six bridesmaids, flowers by the truckload, and 250 guests, including a sit-down dinner with a string quartet and a deejay at the Osprey Country Club."

"Refundable?" I pried.

Wanda shook her head. "Not at this point."

I turned to Jeanette. "That must hurt."

"I don't give a damn about the money," she insisted, then paused. "Although we're not that wealthy, and we've had to borrow money for college, graduate school, and the wedding. But I'm scared for Alicia. This behavior isn't like her."

"Where did she disappear from?" I said.

"Home," Jeanette said with a sniff and dabbed her nose with a tissue. "She was living with us to save money and commuting to the University of South Florida in Tampa."

"Is her car missing, too?"

Her mother nodded.

"Did she say *why* she left?" I asked.

Jeanette rolled her eyes. "She said she wants to *find* herself. After a B.A., M.A., and a Ph.D. in philosophy, how much more self-discovery does she need?"

"What's your take on this?" I asked Wanda.

The wedding planner frowned. "A year ago, when we started making plans, Alicia was enthusiastic, excited. You have to begin making decisions well in advance to carry off a wedding this massive, you know."

I nodded with a grimace. "So my mother and sister have told me. But lately, had Alicia's attitude changed?"

Wanda nodded. "The last few weeks, she seemed different."

"Reluctant?" I suggested.

"Distracted."

"She was finishing her dissertation," Jeanette insisted. "Of course she was distracted."

"What was the subject of her dissertation?" I asked.

Jeanette waved her hand. "Transcendentalism, spiritualism, some such nonsense. She tried explaining it, but I didn't understand a word. But then Alicia's very bright, much smarter than me."

"In the voice mail she left," I said, "was there any sign of coercion in her tone?"

Jeanette shook her head. "She sounded more elated than anything."

"Was her farewell note typed or handwritten?"

"She wrote it on her personal stationery."

"Any signs of tension or anything out of the ordinary in her handwriting or the words she chose?"

Jeanette shook her head. "That's another reason the police won't get involved."

"So you feel reasonably certain her disappearance is her own doing and not the result of kidnapping?"

"Not totally," Jeanette said and added with a frown,

"because it doesn't make sense. Alicia *wants* to marry Garth. Why would she leave? And why won't she answer her phone to talk to Garth or her father and me?"

"Just to be clear," I said, "you want me to find Alicia only to make sure she's all right?"

Jeanette nodded.

I patted Roger, who was getting restless and looking longingly at Wanda's bare, tanned legs. "If I find her, I can't promise she'll come home to go through with the wedding."

Jeanette looked pained. "Understood. But her father and I have to know that she's okay."

She looked even more anguished when I quoted my hourly rate. Wanda, however, seemed unperturbed. Whether I found Alicia or not, the wedding planner's nonrefundable fee was already in the bag.

CHAPTER 2

A few hours later, I paused inside the front door of Dock of the Bay and searched for Bill. The rustic restaurant with its knotty pine walls, decorated with seashells, crab traps and fishnets, overlooked Pelican Bay Marina where Bill lived aboard his cabin cruiser. A blast of cold, air-conditioned air hit me, a welcome change from the stifling heat and humidity that continued to build outside. An afternoon thunderstorm was the only hope for breaking the stifling conditions.

The lunch crowd had barely begun trickling in, but the old Wurlitzer in the bar was already in full swing with Joe Nichols crooning "Tequila Makes Her Clothes Fall Off." The lyrics made me smile. Some liked country music for its melancholy. I loved its sense of humor.

Bill waved from our usual booth and flashed a welcome with the blue-eyed expression that had won my heart two decades ago. I slid onto the bench across from him and ordered raspberry iced tea from the waitress.

I'd spent the remainder of the morning at the office with Jeanette Langston, making lists of Alicia's friends and acquaintances and their addresses. Then I'd taken Roger to my waterfront condo for a walk before settling him in his favorite doggy bed while I joined Bill for an early lunch. This afternoon I would begin the search for the elusive Alicia.

Bill, with his thick white hair, muscular physique, and Beach Boys tan, although ten years my senior, had grown more handsome with age, but I loved him as much if not more for his good heart and happy disposition. We were polar opposites, I an introvert with insecurities and pessimism rooted in my childhood, Bill an extrovert and perennial optimist. No wonder I was consumed with premarital jitters, even though the wedding was months away.

"Busy morning?" he said with that smile that could make me promise him anything.

I filled him in on the runaway bride.

"You think she's lost her nerve?" he asked. "Or is maybe mentally unstable?"

"No hint of mental illness from either her mother

or the wedding planner, but, according to her mother, her behavior's definitely not normal. I should have a better take on why she took off after I talk to her fiancé and some of her friends this afternoon."

I sighed.

Bill narrowed his eyes and studied me with an intensity that made me squirm. "What's wrong, Margaret?"

I could never hide anything from Bill. He read body language better than I read English.

"What makes you think something's wrong?" I hedged.

"Is your mother still on your case about a big wedding?"

"I'll deal with it. As soon as I can screw my courage to the sticking point and confront her."

One part of me yearned for my mother's approval and unconditional love, withheld my entire life, and, illogically, considered the possibility that going along with her wedding plans might produce the desired results. The smart part of me knew better.

"Something has you restless and uneasy." He nodded toward my left hand and the engagement ring he'd given me last Christmas, three aquamarines, my birthstone, set in yellow gold. "Having second thoughts?"

"You know I love you."

He nodded and reached across the table for my hand. "And I know the idea of marriage scares you senseless. If that's what's bothering you—"

"No." I shook my head, then flashed a rueful grin. "I'm willing to give marriage my best shot and praying that my best shot will be good enough."

"Don't sell yourself short. I've been wanting to marry you for twenty years."

I squeezed his hand and released it when the waitress returned with my tea. Bill waited until she'd taken our order and left before continuing. "So, what is bugging you today?"

I tried to get a handle on the vague dissatisfaction I felt so I could put it into words. "I think I need a career change."

He sat back in the booth as if I'd hit him. "You want out of the business? We only started the P.I. firm a few months ago."

I was doing a lousy job of expressing how I felt, primarily because I couldn't really put a name to my discontent.

"Look at us," I said. "You doing background checks on someone's great-aunt Agatha and me chasing down runaway brides. When I was a cop, I at least had the satisfaction of knowing that what I did made a difference."

Bill shook his head. "How quickly you forget."

"What?"

"The futility of being on the job. Long boring hours on patrol or surveillance, following one dead-end lead after another, cases we couldn't crack, and the criminals we collared, only to have them released on technicalities. We didn't always win the good fight for truth, justice and the American way."

"At least I *felt* useful." My mood had blackened this morning with the arrival of Mother's package and worsened with the story of Alicia Langston. I was sliding downward into depression and unable to put on the brakes.

Worry filled Bill's blue eyes. "When's the last time you had a checkup?"

"I don't remember."

"Then it's been too long. Schedule one, okay?"

"But I feel fine."

He cocked an eyebrow. "You've been through a lot recently. A string of murder investigations, the police department's closing, your mother's illness. That much stress can take its toll."

"I'm fine, really. Just having a bad day."

"Then have a checkup for *my* peace of mind, okay? So I won't worry about you."

My late father had been a cardiologist and a firm believer in preventive medicine. As little as I liked being prodded and poked, I knew Bill was right. "I'll schedule a physical, although I don't relish an examination. My current doctor looks younger than Doogie Howser."

Taking me at my word, Bill nodded. "Now, about this career thing."

"I'm open to suggestions."

His eyes lit with devilment. "Have you considered exotic dancing?"

"I'm a bit long in the tooth for that."

"Believe me, my lovely Margaret, no one would be looking at your teeth."

"And I'd meet a whole new class of people." His teasing was already brightening my mood. I couldn't be around Bill for long without feeling better.

"If you're missing police work," he said with more seriousness, "you could apply with the sheriff's office. And Tampa's short a detective now that Abe Mackley's retired."

"Are you trying to get rid of me?" My depression was lifting, only to be replaced by paranoia.

He shook his head. "I'm happy to be working with you, but I want you to be happy, too."

"You're right about the dark side of police work. I'm too old for the long hours and fed up with the political infighting rampant in every department."

"You're forty-nine," he said with a twinkle in his eye, "going on twenty-three. Young enough to do whatever you want. I take it library work is out?"

I'd graduated from college with a degree in library science. When I'd abandoned books and entered the police academy to fight crime, I'd never looked back. "The shock of the peace and quiet of a library job might kill me."

"You could teach at the academy. Or sell real estate. That's hot right now."

Neither profession had any appeal. I shook my head. "I don't have the patience for either."

The waitress returned with our order, and Bill dug into his burger. After chewing and swallowing his first bite, he said, "The bookstore beneath the office is for sale."

"Really?"

"The owners want to move back north. Last year's hurricane season spooked them. You could buy them out, be your own boss."

I paused with a French fry halfway to my mouth. "You're not serious?"

"You love books. You'd be surrounded by them every day."

I considered his suggestion. "And spend all my time directing customers to the cookbook and self-help shelves?" I shook my head. "Where's the challenge in that?"

"Where's the challenge in being a private investigator?"

"It's like working puzzles, such as where is Alicia Langston and why did she run away?" A light dawned as I realized what he'd done. "I'm addicted, aren't I?"

"To solving puzzles? 'Fraid so. More than two decades as a cop will do that to you, a permanent case of 'what's wrong with this picture?'"

"Which is why I'd never be happy doing anything else."

"I didn't say that," he protested.

"But you've made me recognize it." I dug into my burger with gusto, feeling as if a weight had lifted from my shoulders. Bill was my North Star, helping me find my way, especially when frustration caused by my mother knocked me off course.

Bill's cell phone rang and he answered it quickly.

"That was Darcy," he said after he flipped it shut. "Antonio Stavropoulos called the office. He wants to hire us."

"For what?"

"He didn't say, just that he wanted to talk to you about it."

"More work is good," I said with conviction, "as long as it has nothing to do with weddings."

After lunch, I walked from the Dock of the Bay on the south side of the marina across the city park to Sophia's on the north side. Although the temperature had risen into the nineties, an onshore breeze laden with a fresh briny scent made the trek bearable, and I arrived at the upscale restaurant without dissolving into a puddle of sweat.

Sophia's, built to resemble a Venetian palazzo in imitation of John Ringling's Sarasota mansion, perched in pink-stuccoed splendor on the water's edge and brought back a flood of memories. Last fall the restaurant's owner had been one of several victims in a series of murders. Dave Adler, my young partner on the Pelican Bay Police Department, and I, along with help from Bill, had solved the crimes. The last time I'd seen Antonio Stavropoulos had been at Thanksgiving, when he'd asked me to stop by for a box of pastries, a gift of thanks to the department for their hard work.

In the lobby, crowded with patrons waiting to be seated in the luxurious dining room that served world class food, I looked for Antonio, but the maître d's station was empty. I snagged the elbow of a passing waiter, asked for Antonio, and he pointed me down a hall to the manager's office, formerly occupied by Lester Morelli, now awaiting trial for murdering his wife Sophia, among others.

At the end of the hall, I knocked at the door and noted Antonio's name engraved on a brass plate. The maître d' had moved up in the world.

"Enter," a masculine voice with a thick Greek accent called.

I stepped into the office, and Antonio bounded from behind the desk to greet me and offer a chair. The tall, elderly man was dressed as usual in a well-tailored suit with a continental cut and an impeccable white shirt and conservative tie. His gray hair and snowy mustache were neatly trimmed.

"Thank you for coming so quickly," he said. "We have a...ah...situation."

"You're the manager now?" I settled in the chair across from the desk.

Antonio nodded, circled his desk and sat. "Manager and part owner. I bought a half interest from Anastasia Gianakis. She is my silent partner."

Anastasia, Sophia Morelli's aunt, a secondary beneficiary, had inherited the restaurant when I'd proved Lester, Sophia's husband and heir, had killed his wife. The creep, who'd counted on getting everything his dead wife had owned, might end up instead with a death sentence.

"From the crowd in the lobby," I noted, "I'd guess business is good."

"Business is excellent," Antonio said with a nod of satisfaction. "And I want to keep it that way. This new firm of yours, do you handle security?"

"It depends. What kind of security do you have in mind?"

Antonio leaned forward and clasped his long, slender

fingers on the desktop. "You have heard of the Montagues and the Capulets? The Hatfields and McCoys?"

I nodded, wondering where he was headed.

"Well, I have a dinner for two hundred scheduled for the Burnses and the Bakers."

For a moment I drew a blank. Then memory served. "The Pineland Circle Burnses and Bakers?"

He nodded solemnly. "The very same."

"They're having a dinner *together*?"

He nodded again with a grimace. "And I need your help to assure that they do not kill each other and destroy our banquet room in the course of the evening."

"Why would the Burnses and Bakers schedule a dinner together?"

Antonio cocked his head in interest. "Do you know the history of these feuding families?"

"During the time I was with the department, our officers probably responded to more signal twenty-twos at Pineland Circle than all other addresses combined."

"What is this 'signal twenty-two'?"

Police jargon came so naturally to me, I often forgot others weren't fluent. "A disturbance. To put it mildly."

I shook my head. "And it all started over a grapefruit tree."

"Someone was stealing fruit?"

"If only it had been that simple." I could still picture the scene on what should have been a quiet residential cul-de-sac fifteen years ago, with twelve little urchins, all under the age of twelve, six in each family, who seemed to believe their sole purpose on earth was to torment each other. "The children from each family would stand in their respective yards and taunt each other by calling names. The first blow in the battle was struck when the Burns kids began pelting the Baker children with rotten grapefruit from the Burnses' tree."

"Where were their parents?"

"Unfortunately, more often than not, standing on the sidelines, egging them on."

"And the police put a stop to this?"

I shook my head. "Events escalated. The oldest Baker boy chopped down the Burnses' grapefruit tree. The Burnses filed charges. It might have ended there, but the Baker children retaliated by slashing the tires on Mr. Burns's truck and scrawling graffiti over their driveway and sidewalk. The adult Burnses filed more charges, while their kids soaped the Bakers' windows and rolled their trees in toilet paper. Then the Bakers filed charges. This back-and-forth went on for years, often with physical confrontations between the children. It was like gang warfare, but without knives or firearms."

"And the parents continued to encourage it?" Antonio asked in disbelief. "Why did they not move away?"

"The whole situation became a test of wills." Patrol officers had answered calls on Pineland Circle right up until the department had disbanded last February. "The family feuds became a reason for living, a challenge to see who blinked first."

Antonio leaned back in his chair. "How ironic."

"This dinner of yours," I warned, "it's more likely to be World War III."

"That is why I want your firm to provide security to keep the attendees under control."

"Why are they having a joint dinner anyway?" I asked.

"I did not tell you?" He shook his head as if he couldn't believe what he was going to say. "Linda Burns is marrying Kevin Baker and both their extended families will be present at the wedding reception here."

CHAPTER 3

"You don't need security," I said with conviction. "You need Delta Force. Maybe CentCom at MacDill will rent them out."

Antonio's expression fell.

"If you knew about their feud," I asked, "why did you agree to host their reception?"

"I did *not* know. Mrs. Burns exhibited tension and made some hints of disagreement when she came in to book the banquet room and select the menu, but strain is often present between prospective in-laws. I thought nothing more about it until my sous-chef recognized the names on the calendar and alerted me. He lives down the block from them and has witnessed their neighborhood turf wars." Antonio spread his hands in a gesture of helplessness. "By then, the contract was signed."

"I hope it includes a healthy damage deposit."

"So you cannot help me?"

I suppressed a sigh. What was the point of being in business if we couldn't meet the client's needs? "When's the reception?"

"The last Saturday of the month."

I thought for a moment. With Bill and me and Abe Mackley, who'd indicated an interest in working with us after his retirement, I'd have a force of three. And Adler, with one toddler and a new baby on the way, might want to earn some extra cash.

"How many guests did you say?" I asked.

"Two hundred."

"Are you serving liquor?"

Antonio's face paled. "Champagne and an open bar."

Fifty people apiece, in varying stages of hostility and inebriation, for us to keep tabs on. "And exactly what would you expect security to do?"

"Mingle with the guests. Watch for signs of problems. Escort troublemakers from the room to cool off. If they do not, bar them from reentering. And, but only as a last resort, call the police. Sophia's has a reputation to maintain."

Recalling the long history of bad blood between the two families, I recognized the very real potential for someone being seriously hurt, not to mention damage to the restaurant.

"Give me a day or two. I'll see if I can put together a team. If not, I'll find a good security firm to recommend."

Antonio's relief was palpable. "Thank you, Detective Skerritt."

"Just Maggie now," I said and headed for the door. "I'll be in touch."

After leaving Sophia's, I returned to the Dock of the Bay for my ancient Volvo and drove north on Alternate Nineteen. Just south of the country club, I turned into an older and less elegant neighborhood, filled with Spanish-style homes from the thirties and forties with stucco exteriors and clay tile roofs. With almost every square inch of property already built out in the county, these houses, which would once have been affordable to the working class, now sold for over three hundred thousand. Garth Swinburn, Alicia's fiancé, had either inherited his or earned a generous income.

I parked in the driveway beneath the shade of a spreading live oak bearded with Spanish moss and followed a mosaic-tile walk to the front door. With its walls a cheerful Tuscan gold and roof of terra-cotta, the house had a lush lawn and attractive, tropical landscaping. Although decades old, it had been well maintained and had a welcoming appearance, a home most brides would appreciate, so I doubted that disapproval of the real estate had played a part in Alicia's flight.

I rang the doorbell and waited. Jeanette had told me Garth would be here, since he ran his computer consulting business from home. I was beginning to think he'd left to make a house call, when the heavy wooden door with its tiny wrought iron-covered window swung open.

Standing on the threshold was a tall, gangly man in his mid-twenties. His sandy hair stood in unruly peaks, as if he'd recently run his fingers through it, his feet were bare, and he was dressed in khakis and the most obnoxious plaid shirt I'd ever seen. His eyes were glazed with the look of someone who'd just awakened or been pulled from the depths of concentration. With his thick glasses, he reminded me of guys who, in my youth, would have worn plastic pocket protectors and carried slide rules on their belts. *Nerds*, we'd called them. I didn't know if the term was apt in today's lingo, but Garth definitely had a geeky air about him.

Until he smiled. His welcoming look brightened his face and exuded warmth. The kid was a charmer.

"Ms. Skerritt?"

I nodded. "Garth Swinburn?"

"Come in," he said. "Mrs. Langston said I should expect you. Have you found Alicia?"

He sounded so hopeful, I hated to disappoint him. "I don't work quite as fast as those computers of yours. This may take a while."

"Of course." He blushed until the tips of his ears turned red. "Silly of me. I was just hoping—"

"Can you answer a few questions?"

"Sure. Anything to help. Come in."

I stepped through the open door into a completely bare living room. Not even draperies on the windows, just a high sheen on the hardwood floors. He must have seen the surprise in my expression.

"The only room that's furnished is my office," he said. "I even sleep there. I'm waiting for Alicia to decide how she wants to decorate."

From the way he spoke her name, I could tell Garth was crazy about his fiancée.

We crossed the living room, passed through a newly remodeled kitchen and stepped into a sunny family room at the back of the house. Every flat surface was covered with monitors, computers, piles of software, boxes of parts and rolls of cables. The only uncluttered spots were a rolling stenographer's chair and a sofa topped with a pillow and blanket.

Garth tossed the sofa bedding to one side and offered me a seat, then settled into the chair. "I'm worried sick," he said.

"You still haven't heard from Alicia?"

His shoulders drooped, and he shook his head. "I can't believe she'd just walk out without saying *something*. She's not a callous person."

"According to her mother, her note said she was trying to 'find herself.' Maybe she has to figure out what she wants to do."

Garth looked doubtful. "I don't get it."

"You had no clue she was unhappy?"

"She wasn't unhappy," he insisted. "Just the opposite. She seemed to be walking on air. I figured she was glad to be finishing her dissertation and looking forward to our wedding. That's why I'm so worried. I don't believe Alicia left of her own free will."

"How do you explain the voice-mail message and the written note?"

He scratched the tip of his nose. "Someone could have forced her to leave them."

"Did Mrs. Langston share them with you?"

He nodded. "I insisted we call the police."

"You think Alicia left the messages under duress? Could you hear it in her voice, tell it from her writing?"

Garth thought for a moment, then shook his head. "She sounded normal, and her handwriting looked typical."

"Then why your conviction that someone's taken her against her will?"

He confronted me with guileless brown eyes. "Because Alicia wouldn't do this to me or her parents. She knows how much pain it would cause. Like I said, she's not a thoughtless or selfish person."

"When did you last see her?"

"The night before she disappeared. We had dinner at Angellino's."

"What did you talk about?"

His face reddened again. "I did most of the talking. I was excited about new software I'm developing for user-friendly multi-computer interfacing with business applications and told Alicia all about it."

That conversation might have put the girl into a

deep sleep but not necessarily on the run. "And what did Alicia talk about?"

"Alicia's not like most girls."

"How do you mean?"

He scrunched his face as if searching for the right words. "She isn't into fashion and trends."

"Then why the big wedding with all the bells and whistles?"

He grimaced. "Her mother's idea. You know how it is."

Boy, howdy, did I ever. I nodded and tried to ignore the sympathetic clenching in my gut. "So she wasn't looking forward to it?"

Garth shook his head. "But she didn't really mind it too badly. She wants to make her mother happy. Alicia's like that, always thinking of others. And always looking inward, as if material things don't matter." He flushed again. "Since I'm usually neck-deep in my work, we make a good pair. Not exactly social butterflies."

So good a pair that she left? "You were about to tell me her topic of conversation that night."

"Right." He sat with one leg crossed over the other, his ankle resting on his knee, giving me an eye-level view of his bare size-thirteen foot. I contemplated popular mythology and wondered about their sex life but was smart enough to know what *not* to ask.

Garth leaned forward. "Alicia was expounding on one of her favorite themes that night—who am I and why am I here? You ever ask yourself those questions?"

"Only when I've had too much to drink."

He flashed his boyish grin again, reminding me of Adler, another point in Garth's favor. "Until our dinner at Angellino's, Alicia had worried that she'd never find the answers. But that night she said she thought she'd discovered the key."

"Did she say what it was?"

"Nope. Said she didn't want to talk about it further until she was sure."

"Did she say where she'd been, what she'd been doing, who she'd been talking to?"

"Like I said, we talked mostly about me." His expression spasmed with distress. "God, it just hit me. You think that's why she ran away? Because I talk too much about myself?"

I felt sorry for the kid. "I don't know enough about Alicia to form an opinion yet."

"I should have paid more attention to her."

"Don't beat yourself up." He was male, after all. His self-absorption was in his genes. And his jeans. "And don't jump to conclusions. Wait until you've talked to Alicia."

"You have to find her."

"I'm planning on it."

"Have you talked to her friends?"

"Mrs. Langston gave me a list. Anyone in particular I should start with?"

"Julianne Pritchard." He lifted his hand and crossed two fingers. "She and Alicia are like this."

"Have you talked to Julianne?"

Garth nodded. "She says she doesn't know where Alicia is."

"She might know other facts that will help. I have her address."

Garth checked his watch. "Julianne's probably still at work. She waits tables at Hooters in Clearwater."

His worry was palpable, so I tried to reassure him. "Julianne may know something that will lead me to Alicia."

"I hope so." His expression turned grim. "If not, my gut tells me Alicia's in real trouble."

CHAPTER 4

I left Garth's house, headed east to U.S. 19, then turned south. What had, in my childhood, been a bucolic drive along a country road through pastures and citrus groves was now six lanes under construction of wall-to-wall traffic hell. Our local politicians referred to it as progress. I figured for every minute I spent on that route, another hair on my head turned gray.

I exited at the cloverleaf at Gulf-to-Bay Boulevard and turned left onto another six-lane nightmare. Between tourists who hadn't a clue where they were going and the over-ninety retirees whose licenses should have been revoked years earlier, my commute reminded me of the bumper-car rides at the county fair, minus the element of fun. I said a silent prayer of thanks that my old Volvo was built like a tank and considered the odds. I'd been rear-ended two months ago, so statistically I wasn't due for another crash soon, unless I turned out to be one of those unfortunate anomalies.

With a sense of relief, I parked in Hooters' lot and turned off the engine. Every time I survived a drive through the county, I felt the urge to carve a notch in my steering wheel.

The Hooters parking lot and restaurant were almost empty at mid-afternoon. The lunch crowd had left and happy hour hadn't started. I stepped into the dim interior and inhaled the odor of stale beer, fried onions and cooking grease while my eyes adjusted. A large-screen television over the bar was tuned to a golf tournament with the commentary muted. Raucous music blared through the sound system. The place lived up to its slogan of "Delightfully Tacky Yet Unrefined." I couldn't have said it better myself.

"Can I help you?"

Perky was the only word to describe the waitress who greeted me. About five foot five with long legs, tiny waist and generous breasts, all accentuated by the Hooters uniform of hip-hugger shorts and cropped, tight T-shirt, she could have been a cheerleader for the NFL. With long, straight hair, however, this was no dumb blonde. Intelligence shone in her clear gray eyes.

"I'm looking for Julianne Pritchard."

"That's me."

"I'm Maggie Skerritt, a private investigator. Jeanette Langston hired me to find Alicia."

"Oh." Uncertainty replaced her welcoming look.

"Is there a booth where we can talk?"

"Why do you want to talk to me?" Reluctance edged her voice, not exactly the response I'd been expecting.

"Garth Swinburn said you and Alicia are close. I thought you might have some clue to where she's gone."

She looked over her shoulder, then back at me, obviously uncomfortable. "I could lose my job, talking to you here."

I glanced around the room, empty of patrons except for a middle-aged man, drinking beer and eating pretzels at the bar. "I'd hate to be a stumbling block in your illustrious career."

"This job is only temporary, but I need it until I get a permanent one. I have an accounting degree," she added, getting huffy, "and have interviewed with several firms."

Take that, you lowly private investigator.

Unintimidated by the budding number cruncher, I plowed on. "This won't take long."

With a sigh of resignation and the apparent realization that I would stick to her like a tick on a dog until I got answers, Julianne led me toward the rear of the dining room and called to the bartender, "I'm taking my break."

I slid into a booth in the back corner and Julianne sat opposite me as if on springs, ready to bounce off at the first excuse. Her gaze flitted to the wall behind me, out the window, down to the floor. Anywhere except looking me in the eye. I didn't have to be a trained investigator to know a guilty conscience when I saw it.

"So," I said in a casual tone that I hoped would put her at ease, "tell me about Alicia."

"What about her?" Julianne's gray eyes narrowed with belligerence.

"Her mother and Garth claim you're her best friend."

"So?" She packed a truckload of hostility into one little word.

"So any idea where she may have gone?"

"Not a clue." Her glance to the right, again avoiding my eyes, assured me she was lying through her lovely pearly whites.

For a moment I said nothing, allowing the falsehood to hang in the air and watching Julianne fidget.

"Okay," I said after letting her stew in her fib until she looked ready to jump out of her skin, "let's cut the crap. I don't have time for this and you have to get back to work. You know where she is, don't you?"

Julianne jutted her chin upward. "You're not the police. I don't have to tell you anything."

"Fine." I shrugged with a no-skin-off-my-back attitude. "As long as you're certain she's safe."

Julianne's bravado evaporated. "What are you saying?"

"I'm not a cop now, but I was one for twenty-three years. I've seen the terrible things that can happen to a young woman when she's cut off from her family and friends." I shrugged and started to push to my feet. "But as long as you're convinced she's okay."

"Wait!"

I eased back onto the bench.

Julianne looked ready to cry. "I promised Alicia I'd keep her secret."

"From everything I've been told, Alicia is a caring young woman. Why would she want to keep her whereabouts secret from those who love her most?"

"They made her sign a covenant that she wouldn't tell anyone."

"They?" I watched Julianne's inner debate between ratting on her friend and worry over Alicia's safety play out across her face.

Finally, she exhaled a deep breath, the battle won. "Grove Spirit House."

I knew where it was, in the middle of one of the last remaining orange groves in Pelican Bay, but other than the fact that it was some type of religious retreat, I knew nothing about the recently built facility. Most folks in town had been relieved when the new owner hadn't cleared the grove for development. After learning that the greenbelt would be spared, interest in the property and its owner had faded.

"Maybe," I suggested, "you'd better start at the beginning."

The front door opened and a crowd of young men entered and staked out two tables in the middle of the room.

Julianne stood. "I have to get back to work."

"Can I talk to you later?"

Her attitude seemed torn, but whether between the desire to get rid of me or to share her concerns about her friend, I couldn't tell.

"My shift ends at eight," she said. "I'll be home by eight-thirty."

"I have your address. I'll see you then."

To avoid further thrills on U.S. 19, I took Old Coachman Road after leaving Hooters, then threaded my way along backstreets into the eastern fringes of Pelican Bay and the entrance to Grove Spirit House. The twenty-acre enclave of orange trees was surrounded on three sides by subdivisions and the fourth by a large lake. The only access was a driveway of crushed shells that had once led through the groves to a rustic fruit stand, roofed in palm fronds, where the previous owners had sold fresh citrus, jellies and orange-blossom honey.

Today an eight-foot chain-link fence ringed the entire property, and I doubted its purpose was to discourage fruit theft. Although unripe oranges adorned many of the trees, the branches weren't pruned, and the rows between the trees, filled with high weeds, clearly hadn't been cultivated in years. Whoever owned Grove Spirit House had a serious chunk of change, because the undeveloped land alone, a scarcity in the county, was worth millions, whether the grove was productive or not.

I parked in front of an electronic gate that blocked the entrance to the drive and got out of the car. An intercom was attached to the right of the gate, and I caught sight of a surveillance camera mounted on a nearby utility pole. I punched the call button on the intercom and waited a few minutes, but no one answered.

I pushed the call button again.

"Yes?" The voice was female, low and throaty.

"I'm here to see Alicia Langston."

"Who?"

"Alicia Langston," I repeated.

"I'm sorry." She didn't sound sorry. "We don't reveal the names of our guests. And we don't admit anyone without an appointment."

"Then I'd like to make an appointment."

I waited, but the woman made no reply. I hit the call button again with no results. Whoever had answered had either left the intercom or was being purposely incommunicado.

That really ticked me off. When good manners failed to obtain results, I had no qualms about resorting to threats, but I reined in my temper. If activities at Grove Spirit House were nefarious, I didn't want to raise their defenses before I'd had a chance to snoop further.

I keyed the intercom. "How do I make an appointment?"

Sultry Voice returned. "The office opens at nine tomorrow morning. But appointments are only for participants in our retreats."

"Can you at least put Alicia on the intercom, so I can assure her family that she's all right?"

This time, Sultry Voice said nada.

By now, alarm bells were jangling in my brain. The type of exclusiveness practiced at Grove Spirit House was usually one of two things: the privilege of extreme wealth or the secretiveness of something underhanded. Because neither Alicia nor her family was filthy rich, my money was on deceit, and my investigative nose smelled the stench of a cult.

Closing time was fast approaching when I returned to the office. Darcy was clearing the top of her desk.

"Can you check something on Google for me before you leave?" I asked.

A true technophobe, I avoided computers whenever possible. And irritated Bill by refusing to own a cell phone. Now that I was no longer on the police force, I didn't even carry a beeper. I loved the heady freedom of being electronically disconnected.

Darcy poised her hands above the keyboard. "What do you need?"

"Everything you can find on Grove Spirit House here in Pelican Bay, including a phone number."

"I'm on it. Your messages are on your desk."

Darcy concentrated on her monitor and I went into my office. A note from Bill said he'd pick me up at my condo sometime after six to take me to dinner. The second message was from Caroline, who'd dropped by the office while I was out, hoping to discuss bridal gowns. I felt a wave of relief at dodging that bullet.

Darcy came in with a manila folder and handed it to me. "I printed out everything I could find. The phone number's in there." She shook her head. "Sounds like one strange outfit."

"How strange?"

"Fasting, bathing naked in the lake, sitting for hours in a smokehouse, beating drums, communing with spirits. *Cleansing*, they call it. I call it nuts. Good way to get eaten alive by mosquitoes and alligators."

According to the signals my gut was sending, mosquitoes and alligators weren't the only predators at Grove Spirit House. The sooner I found Alicia, the better.

Back at my condo an hour later, I watched Roger scarf the last of his kibble and empty his water dish. How one little dog could drink twice his weight in water, I'd never understand. I'd already taken him for a long walk along the waterfront and planned to read the file on Grove Spirit House while I waited for Bill to take me to dinner.

Before I could make myself comfortable, a knock sounded at the front door. Expecting Bill, I opened it without checking the peephole.

Caroline breezed past, down the hall and into my living room. She clutched a stack of bridal magazines in one arm and held a Neiman Marcus shopping bag overflowing with fabric samples in her other hand.

"Finally," she said with a note of triumph. "We've got to plan this wedding."

I gazed past her, expecting to see my mother bringing up the rear. The parking lot and front walkway were empty. The only good thing about Caroline's visit was that she was alone.

With nowhere to run and no place to hide, I followed her into the living room.

CHAPTER 5

Emitting a joyous woof, Roger bounded from the kitchen and raced straight for Caroline's legs, clad in expensive sheer stockings, even in the summer heat.

"Don't even think about it, pal." Her commanding tone stopped Roger in his tracks. My sister had been subjected to his amorous ways before and deemed them socially unacceptable.

In her eyes, Roger and I were at least in the same boat. Seven years my senior, Caroline was Mother's perfect daughter. Refined, elegant and oozing social graces, my sister was everything I wasn't: married to a wealthy, prominent man, president of the Art Guild, mother and grandmother, and dressed to the nines every time she stepped outside her door.

Caroline also thrived on being in charge and, unfortunately, my distant nuptials now topped her to-do list.

"I don't have time for this now," I said. "Bill will be here any minute to take me to dinner."

Caroline sank onto the sofa and began arranging magazines and fabric swatches on the coffee table. "Good. We can get his opinion."

Desperate to be rid of her, I pointed to the gowns on the magazine covers. "Isn't it bad luck for the groom to see the bride's dress before the ceremony?"

Caroline was a stickler for tradition but not to be deterred. "Good thinking. Lock the door, and when he comes, don't let him in until I've hidden what we've selected."

Unconcerned with superstition, I left the door un-latched. To my sister's credit, however, I had to admit that her heart was in the right place. She just couldn't get her head around the fact that I couldn't care less about wedding dresses or any other aspect of an elab-orate ceremony. She lived to shop and believed every-one else shared her enthusiasm.

"Why don't you leave those?" I suggested. "Give me a chance to look through them and get back to you."

The look she shot me reminded me so much of Mother that I shivered.

"Now," she said, "back to business. What about white?"

"What about it?"

She cupped her chin in her hand and studied me with a frown. "You are older and probably…uh…more experienced than most brides—" Her expression brightened. "But virginal isn't a requirement for wearing white these days."

"Not only do I not want white—"

"Good! That's a beginning." She grabbed a magazine from the top of the stack. "Here's a Vera Wang creation that would suit you. And plum is the hot new color for brides."

"Plum? As in purple? It turns my skin yellow. If I appear in public in plum, one of Daddy's doctor friends will place my name on the waiting list for a liver transplant."

"Not a problem. It comes in other colors."

Arguing with Caroline was like pushing on a rope.

She thrust the magazine into my hands. "See? What do you think?"

I studied the picture of a skinny model with flawless shoulders dressed in a strapless fitted bodice and enough fabric in her billowing skirt to clothe a small school and shook my head, as much in disbelief as negation. "Much too formal for what Bill and I have in mind, and—my God! Five thousand dollars for a *dress?*" I struggled for breath. "You've got to be kidding. I paid less than that for my first car."

Caroline waved her fingers in a breezy gesture of dismissal. "Mother's picking up the tab. She can afford it."

"Caroline," I said in my firmest tone, "Bill and I want our wedding to be uncomplicated, simple—"

"*Elegant* is the word you're looking for."

"No, I was going for *small*. Very small. Try minuscule."

She looked shocked. "But it can't be small. Mother's planning for eight hundred."

My knees gave way and I sank into the nearest chair. "I don't even *know* eight hundred people."

"They're Mother's friends."

"But this is *my* wedding."

"Would you deny your elderly mother the pleasure of seeing her daughter married in appropriate style?" When Logic Fails, Apply Guilt was Caroline's motto, aptly learned at dear old mom's knee.

"Appropriate style?" I sputtered with frustration. "What you two have in mind is more like a three-ring circus."

Anger flashed briefly across Caroline's perfectly made-up face. She took a deep breath before speaking. "I know you're suffering from premarital jitters, but—"

"The only thing making me jittery is the prospect of a wedding fit for Donald Trump." Desperation made my tone sharper than I'd intended and I felt the stirring of hives beneath my skin, usually brought forth only by having to deal with homicide.

Caroline's smile turned catlike. "Trump's on the guest list."

I groaned and buried my face in my hands.

At the sound of Bill's car turning into the parking lot, Roger yelped with joy, bounded to the front door, and did his canine version of a happy dance.

"Bill's here." I was thankful for the excuse to give my sister the boot. "No time to hide those bride thingies. You'd better take them with you."

Caroline hurriedly stuffed swatches into the shopping bag and gathered up the magazines. "We'll need to reschedule."

How about twenty years from now? "I'll check my calendar at the office and get back to you," I lied.

Caroline bustled out the front door and passed Bill on the walk.

"Hey, Caroline." Bill greeted her with more warmth than she deserved under the circumstances.

"Hi, Bill. Got to run." She hunched her shoulders to hide the magazines as if they held secrets vital to national security and scurried to her car.

When Bill came inside, I threw my arms around him. "Thank God. Saved by the Bill."

He kissed me, then leaned back to study my face. "Still waging the Battle of the Bride?"

I nodded. "It's a standoff. The enemy won't admit defeat and I refuse to surrender."

Bill shook his leg to shed Roger, an equal-opportunity humper. "Maybe you need new rules of engagement."

"Engagement is what started this war in the first place."

"We could launch a preemptive strike. Pack your bag. We'll elope."

Panic seized me. I wanted to marry Bill, but I wasn't ready. "Not tonight. I have to wash my hair."

He shook his head and laughed.

"You think this is funny?" I said. "Today I learned that Mother's planning to invite Donald Trump to our wedding. They serve together on several charity boards."

"We can handle Donald," Bill assured me with a hug. "He seems like a nice guy."

"Can you handle half the civilized world? So far Mother's guest list is at eight hundred."

Bill's confident expression wavered. "I need a drink. Bring Roger. I know just the place."

I sipped a vodka-and-tonic slowly to make it last. Since I was driving to interview Julianne Pritchard after supper, one drink was my limit.

Roger curled in my lap while I lounged in a teak reclining chair on the rear deck of the *Ten-Ninety-Eight*. Bill manned the grill. Upon retiring from the Tampa Police Department several years ago, Bill had bought the cabin cruiser, named it for the police code for "mission completed," and moved aboard. After we'd closed on our house, a renovated Cape Cod in Dave Adler's neighborhood, Bill had suggested we move into it together, but I'd insisted we wait until after the wedding. My decision was one part knowing how much Bill loved living on his boat, another part my belief in old-fashioned values, and the biggest part my continuing reluctance to take that last giant step toward commitment.

The tantalizing aroma of grouper and an assortment of vegetables mixed with the briny scent of the breeze off the water. Bill turned the food on the grill, grabbed a beer and settled into the chair beside mine. His customary contented expression had disappeared, and the grim lines in his face made him appear older.

"Don't worry," I said. "I won't let Mother and Caroline go through with their plans. It's a long time until February and eventually they'll get the message."

"I know." He leaned back in his chair and stared across the sound toward the barrier islands and the rapidly descending sun, but his dark mood remained.

"Then what's troubling you?" With a jolt of panic, I wondered if Bill was having second thoughts about marrying me. My reluctance to commit was rooted in my feelings of inadequacy, but I'd never doubted how much I loved him. Losing him would be more than I could bear.

He sighed. "I got a hit today on the background checks I've been doing for the Historical Society."

A mixture of relief and surprise rushed through me. "One of your little old ladies has a record?"

He took a long pull at his beer and nodded. "Shoplifting."

"Have you told the museum director?"

Bill shook his head. "And I'm not going to."

"Why?" Bill was the most ethical person I knew, so his refusal didn't make sense. "Isn't that what we volunteered for?"

He leaned toward me with pain-filled eyes. "I talked to her. Bessie Lassiter is eighty-four, lives with her hundred-year-old sister, Violet, and has only their paltry Social Security checks as income. She was caught shoplifting in a grocery store. She was stealing food because she'd run out of funds before the end of the month."

"And some heartless judge convicted her?"

"But let her off with a warning and probation."

"That's so sad. Is there something we can do for her?"

"She won't accept help," Bill said with a shake of his head. "I tried to give her money, but she said her pride is all she has left, and she refuses to accept charity. I hate to think how many elderly are out there in her situation, not having enough money for housing, utilities, groceries and medicine. And the irony is, the food she stole wasn't for herself but for her sister. She said she would have done without, but she couldn't let her sister starve."

I felt sympathy for the old ladies and wanted to do something. "Give Darcy all the info you have on the women tomorrow," I suggested. "Have her check into government assistance programs for seniors."

"I doubt they'll accept help."

"I'm sure they've paid taxes all their lives," I said. "We'll convince them that they're entitled."

He spanned the distance between us and squeezed my hand. "That's a good idea. We'll try it. Now tell me about your day."

I related Antonio Stavropoulos's desire to hire Pelican Bay Investigations for security for the Burns-Baker wedding reception, and Bill frowned again. "Sounds like one huge domestic disturbance."

He didn't have to say more. A domestic disturbance is every police officer's worst nightmare, replete with hot tempers, high passions and, too often, drunkenness and weapons. A drug-crazed husband with a machete had attacked Bill during the first year we'd worked as partners for the Tampa PD. I'd been forced to shoot the man to save Bill's life, the only time in more than twenty-three years as a law enforcement officer that I'd discharged my weapon.

So I understood Bill's reluctance to involve us in

a family feud. "Do you know a security firm I can recommend?"

Bill thought for a moment. "I hate to let Antonio down. If we can get Abe Mackley and Adler to help out, maybe we can keep a lid on trouble. I can do some reconnoitering in the days before the wedding to sniff out potential problems."

"I thought I was supposed to be the workaholic half of this couple," I said.

He shrugged. "You are the one who's heading out for an interview tonight after a full day's work."

"Why take Antonio's offer?"

"If we can put together the right team, we'll have the experience to handle whatever happens. A lot of security firms hire muscle and neglect the brains."

I batted my eyelashes. "Are you telling me you love me for my mind?"

Bill leaned closer. "That and the rest of you. Come here. I'll show you."

"I wouldn't do that if I were you."

He blinked in surprise. "Why not?"

I stifled a laugh at his look of disappointment and pointed to flames rising from the grill. "Because the grouper's burning."

CHAPTER 6

After a meal of blackened grouper, I left Roger with Bill and drove east along Main past the quaint antique shops, chic restaurants and martini bars of downtown. The meandering street of early twentieth-century buildings, lined with brick sidewalks, old-fashioned street lamps and tropical landscaping eventually widened to six lanes edged with strip malls, funeral homes, banks, pharmacies and grocery stores. With sundown fast approaching, traffic had thinned. I took only minutes to reach the turnoff to the apartment complex, tucked behind a bowling alley, where Julianne Pritchard lived.

She answered my knock at the door of her second-floor apartment and invited me in. Her living room, furnished in an assortment of used furniture and bookcases made from boards and concrete blocks, was neat and tidy. A closer look revealed wall art hung at precise levels, furniture arranged at perfect right angles,

books shelved according to height and color. If her cal-
culations were as orderly as her housekeeping, Julianne had the makings of a great accountant.

Dressed in a tunic top, shorts and flip-flops, she had
scrubbed off the heavy makeup she'd worn at work and
looked years younger, almost vulnerable, and worried,
too. She offered me a chair, then curled her bare legs
under herself on the sofa.

"I've been thinking about what you said," she began.

Deciding to let her do the talking, I nodded.

"Especially your question about whether Alicia is
safe or not. I know she's at Grove Spirit House, but
the place seems bizarro."

Having read the file Darcy had printed out from the
Web site, I decided even *bizarro* was a tad mild, but I
nodded again.

Julianne twisted a strand of hair around one finger.
"The only reason Alicia went there originally was to
gather information for her dissertation. She was re-
searching how people find meaning in their lives. But
she was mesmerized by The Teacher."

"The teacher?"

"That's what they call the guy who's in charge of
the place."

"What's his real name?"

"Dunno. Neither did Alicia. She always referred to him as The Teacher with a touch of awe, as if the words should be in capitals and flashing lights."

"What did she find so hypnotic about him?"

"She said he looks like a statue of a Greek God come to life."

"Anything besides his looks?"

Julianne made a face. "Alicia's big on spirituality. She said this guy touches her in ways she'd never imagined."

"Literally?"

Julianne shook her head. "Her soul, her spirit. Sounded like a bunch of crap to me, but Alicia was over the moon. She's certain he has the answers to questions she's been asking all her life, but he said she has to submit to him to find them."

"Submit?" I didn't like the sound of it. Instead of The Teacher, I was thinking Snake Oil Salesman and feeling my skin crawl.

"I told her she was crazy," Julianne said, "but she wouldn't listen. The Teacher said if she wanted to enter Grove Spirit House, she had to renounce the world, that she couldn't tell anyone where she is, and she would have to remain incommunicado until her training is over."

That kind of secrecy usually spelled trouble. "Then why did she tell you where she'd be?"

"She was afraid if she told her folks or Garth, they'd keep her from entering. She thought she could trust me. Look, Alicia's not a complete nutcase. She knew better than to disappear totally without anyone knowing where she's gone. You know, in case her parents got sick or were in an accident or something." Julianne wrinkled her face in distress. "I promised I wouldn't tell, but after you questioned whether she was safe, I started thinking."

Too bad Alicia hadn't done the same. The Teacher's charisma had probably short-circuited her brain. "Does The Teacher provide all this enlightenment free of charge?"

Julianne shook her head. "Garth will be really pissed. Alicia cleaned out their joint account where they'd been saving for their honeymoon."

My bad feelings about Grove Spirit House were growing exponentially. "Did Alicia say how long this training is supposed to take?"

"The Teacher said it would depend on how receptive she is."

And, I thought, on how long the money lasted.

"You'll check on her, won't you?" Julianne asked.

"That's what I promised her mother." And I'd check out this Teacher, too, who sounded more like a con man than a spiritual leader.

When I drove away from Julianne's apartment, I couldn't help thinking that what Jeanette Langston might need wasn't a private eye but a deprogrammer.

By ten the next morning, I was back at the electronic gate at Grove Spirit House, poking the intercom button. I'd had Darcy call earlier to make an appointment. She'd told the woman who'd answered their phone that I was a potential applicant and assured her that I could afford the entrance fee, a whopping sum big enough to choke a goat. Darcy had laid it on thick, hinting that I had money to burn and implying their fee was insignificant. The retreat's receptionist fell all over herself scheduling the first appointment possible.

Remembering the surveillance camera that had given a good view of me and my car yesterday, I'd talked my brother-in-law into trading vehicles for the morning and hoped the opulence of Hunt's new Town Car would create the illusion of wealth. In place of my usual jeans, casual shirt and sneakers, I wore a wide-brimmed hat, sunglasses, too much makeup, high-heeled sandals dug from the depths of my closet and a designer bias-cut sundress Mother had given me for my birthday, which, under normal circumstances, I wouldn't be caught dead in. Its fabric clung so revealingly, I had to carry my gun in my handbag. A glimpse in the mirror as I left the office had assured me my disguise was effective. I looked like a younger version of my sister.

"Yes?" Sultry Voice answered the intercom.

"Priscilla Skerritt," I said in my best imitation of Mother's elegant but condescending voice, a fitting choice since I'd also appropriated her name. If this operation was a scam, The Teacher was looking for wealth and likely to do some research. And in Pelican Bay, they didn't come any wealthier than dear old mom.

The intercom clicked. "Are you here for the cleansing?"

I'd showered at home, but what the heck. "Yes, I have an appointment."

"Proceed to the end of the drive and turn left. Park in front of the main pavilion. I'll meet you there."

The gate clicked and glided open with an electronic whir. I slid behind the wheel of the Lincoln and eased through the entrance. In the rearview mirror, I watched the gate close behind me, like a door slamming on a prison cell.

Shaking off the creeps the place was giving me, I studied the lay of the land. The swaths of mown grass on either side of the shell drive were the sole signs of habitation. The fruit trees had been neglected, their only apparent purpose to serve as a privacy buffer for the compound.

The drive ended at an expanse of lawn that stretched to the edge of a large lake, ringed by cypress swamps and wetlands that provided further seclusion. A road to the right led to a grouping of a dozen tiki-style huts. I turned left and parked in front of a building that reminded me of an oversize Japanese teahouse, framed by graceful palms and bird of paradise in full flower. A stylized water fountain of sculpted bronze and rock centered the pea-gravel path that led to the pavilion with its sliding walls of woven bamboo pushed open to the breeze. I could see through the building to the lake.

A tall, willowy woman with long, satiny dark hair waited on the top step. She was dressed in a tie-dyed caftan and matching headband that gave me flash-backs to the hippies of my youth.

When I reached her, she bowed in Asian fashion, her expression inscrutable. "Welcome to Grove Spirit House. I am Celeste. Follow me."

Before I could reply, she turned and led me into the center of the airy pavilion, furnished only with floor cushions and hanging lamps of burning incense that made me want to sneeze.

"Wait, please. The Teacher will be here shortly to evaluate you."

"Evaluate?"

"To determine if you are worthy of entry."

More likely to check the status of my bank account. Too many years as a cop had made me cynical. "I'll wait."

Celeste didn't offer a cushion and I didn't take one. Unaccustomed to both high heels and sitting on the floor, I feared, once down, I'd have trouble regaining my feet. If The Teacher was the con man I feared, I didn't want to place myself at a disadvantage if a fast escape was necessary.

"Priscilla?"

I jumped at the sound of a strong, seductive male voice and pivoted to find a man standing directly behind me. With the grace of a large cat and bare feet, he'd entered without my hearing.

"And you are?" I asked.

"I am The Teacher," he said in the same weighty tone and lack of humility that Louis XIV must have uttered, *"L'État, c'est moi."*

Julianne had told me that Alicia had described him as the statue of a Greek god come to life. Teach had the physique and either a natural olive complexion or a fabulous bronze tan, but there all resemblance to Greek deity ended. Well over six feet tall, he was dressed in loose white cotton trousers and a long white tunic. With diamond studs winking in each earlobe and a shaved head, he looked more like Mr. Clean. His eyes were big and brown with a bedroom appeal an unsuspecting woman could drown in. Suspicious as hell, I was in no danger.

"And what do you teach?" I injected what I hoped was an appropriate amount of respect into the question.

I wasn't so much interested in his answer as using the delay to survey the compound through the pavilion's open doors. I saw no signs of vehicles or other guests. The interior of a gazebo near the lake was partially hidden by a flame vine that grew over the structure. A gravel path led off to the left toward two large buildings, one like the pavilion in which I stood, the other's roof barely visible through an undergrowth of saw palmettos and wax myrtle.

"I instruct our novices how to tap into and become one with the Universal Spirit," Teach said without humility. And with a straight face.

Unimpressed by his claim of metaphysical hacking, I feigned interest. "And how does that work?"

"I can tell that you are troubled." His voice was soothing, beguiling, hypnotic. "You are facing a major challenge in your life."

I could see how he reeled his victims in. His compassionate tone and commiserating expression would have had a truly distressed person spilling her guts. I played along. "I am getting married soon."

"And you aren't certain it's the right choice?"

I wasn't going there. "How can this Universal Spirit help?"

He closed his eyes, as if in a trance. "When you are one with the Universe, you see and know all things, past, present, future."

Since that claim covered pretty much everything, I nodded. If this guy was for real, he should have made a killing in the stock market, the lottery and at the racetrack, and wouldn't have to be fleecing unsuspecting women.

"How many novices are there?"

My question jarred him from his reverie and he opened his eyes. "Only one at present."

"Celeste?"

He shook his head. "Celeste has attained the Fifth Level of Enlightenment and is my personal assistant. However, a retreat is scheduled for this weekend when ten more novices will arrive."

"You have only one staff member for a complex this size?"

"Hector maintains the grounds, but he lives in town and comes only one day a week. Our novices do the other chores and find their work an enlightenment. And you will find complete privacy and serenity here."

Teach flashed me a look that would have melted a more vulnerable woman. "With Hector and the others not arriving until Friday, that will give us a few days to work alone together. I can take you far in that time."

"To the Fifth Level?"

The guy oozed sexuality like a film star. I had the

feeling he was thinking more along the lines of third base or home plate.

My question made him smile. "To reach the Fifth Level, one must study for years. But the journey of a thousand miles begins with the first step."

Which probably meant a hefty check with more to follow.

"I'm not sure," I stalled. "It's a huge commitment."

"And one that will change your life forever," he said with a solemn nod.

Losing a fortune to a charlatan would be a jolt, I agreed silently.

"Before I make up my mind," I said, "could you show me around?"

His hesitation was so brief, I might have missed it if I hadn't been gauging his every reaction.

"Is there a problem?" I said.

"Only a small matter, but it is the custom here."

I recalled Darcy's description of participants skinny dipping in the lake and, afraid he'd request that I disrobe, had almost decided to blow my cover when he added, "We ask that you remove your shoes. The ground of Grove Spirit House is sacred."

Since the stilettos were killing my feet, I hastened

to comply. Luckily, unlike my sister, I refused to torture myself with panty hose in the June heat, so my feet were truly bare. I stifled a moan of pleasure and flexed my aching toes and arches.

With the strap of my bag over my right shoulder for easy access to my weapon and my shoes dangling in my left hand, I followed Teach out of the pavilion.

He turned left and led me along a pea-gravel path toward another Asian-style building whose sliding walls were open to the summer breeze that did little to dispel the high humidity or swarms of gnats, mosquitoes and deer flies. Screen doors, walls and air-conditioning were apparently an impediment to communing with the Universal Spirit.

"This," he explained, "is the dining pavilion."

Low tables surrounded by cushions filled one end of the single room. The other end was hidden by a large screen that reached almost to the open rafters.

"What's over there?" I didn't wait for an answer but strode across the floor and around the screen before he could restrain me.

The screen hid a kitchen with high-end stainless steel appliances, teak cabinets and limestone countertops. A young woman in an ankle-length white robe stood at a double sink, washing green peas in a colander. She was tall and slender with long blond hair partially covered by a white kerchief.

"Hello," I said.

She turned, and I recognized Alicia Langston from the photographs her mother had given me.

"She must not speak," Teach ordered.

"Why not?"

"As an initiate, she has taken a vow of silence, the better to commune with the Universal Spirit."

Alicia smiled, but not at me. She appeared enchanted by her mentor and worshipped him with her hazel eyes. Otherwise, she looked healthy and happy. She definitely wasn't sending any kind of signal that she wished to be rescued and was obviously there of her own free will.

Poor Garth was flat out of luck. And his honeymoon savings.

"You may resume your duties, Starshine," Teach said gently.

Alicia blushed and turned back to rinsing her peas.

"Starshine?" I said. "That's an unusual name."

With a firm hand on my elbow, he guided me away from Alicia, through the kitchen, out of the dining pavilion and on to the lawn. "Each novice sheds her former name to symbolize leaving her old life behind and is given a name to represent her new calling."

"What about Celeste?"

"She, too, rejected her former life. I chose Celeste for her because it means Heaven."

"And what would my name be?"

"That will depend on what talents I uncover." His gaze was hot and intimate, and I squelched a shudder at its obvious implications.

As a diversion, I pointed across the lawn to the tiki huts that resembled picnic shelters. "What are those?"

"Living quarters."

"What's the Universal Spirit got against climate control?"

His smile was both superior and condescending. "One must remove all traces of one's former existence and commune with nature to join with the Universe."

In other words, suffering was good for you. "Do you bathe in the lake?"

"Every day."

"What about the gators?"

"You must have faith that the Universe will protect you."

Decades as a cop had taught me that the universe

could be a harsh and dangerous place. And a pair of beady eyes, set wide apart and visible above the surface of the lake about twenty feet from shore, informed me that the alligator that lurked there was at least ten feet long. I doubted, however, that Teach would let anything eat his meal tickets. Unless the gator had lost its fear of people as a result of being hand-fed by idiots, a too common practice in the state, a splashing crowd of naked novices would scare it off.

"Will you be joining us, Priscilla?" He spoke the name like a caress.

"I need to think about it," I lied.

I considered the possibility that Teach wasn't a con man, but a true believer in his unusual philosophy. The vibes he'd been emitting insisted otherwise, and his next words clinched my assessment.

"You could make a deposit to hold a place open for you."

"How much of a deposit?"

"A thousand dollars."

I restrained myself from gasping. To someone of Mother's wealth, a thousand bucks was pocket change.

He noted my hesitation and added quickly, "You could write a check."

I shook my head. "I don't want my personal assistant or accountant knowing about this. Let me run to the bank and bring you a cash deposit after lunch."

His grin stretched ear to ear. "Even better."

After lunch, I drove to Jeanette Langston's house to report my findings. Despite her disclaimer of wealth, the Langstons lived in an upscale neighborhood near the waterfront. A late model Beemer was parked in the driveway of their impressive home, built in Key West style. Her husband, Richard, had a drilling operation that had struck it rich. He was a dentist who specialized in root canals.

Jeanette answered the door. She wore a bathing suit with a matching sarong and sandals. "I was out by the pool. Join me and tell me everything."

Having had enough hot, humid air for one day, I'd have preferred to remain in the air-conditioning but followed her through a broad, high-ceilinged hallway to a spacious covered lanai at the back of the house. She offered me a seat at a wicker table, removed a pitcher of tea from an under-the-counter fridge in the outdoor kitchen and poured me a glass.

A row of ceiling fans stirred the muggy air, and

huge palms and ficus trees in terra-cotta pots provided shade from the afternoon sun.

Jeanette sat across from me and clutched her glass in both hands. "You've found Alicia?"

I nodded. "And she's fine, just like her messages said."

"Thank God. Where is she?"

"At a religious retreat right here in Pelican Bay."

"But why?" Jeanette appeared dazed. "We're Episcopalians."

I related every detail of my visit with The Teacher and my brief encounter with Alicia, sticking to the facts and omitting my suspicions.

Jeanette, however, was no dummy. "This stinks of a scam."

"It's possible."

"You have to get Alicia out of there."

I shook my head. "I can't. She's an adult and entered Grove Spirit House of her own free will. She would have to be removed by force, and I don't have that authority."

"I can't just let her throw her life away." Jeanette's grip tightened on her glass until I feared it would break. "There has to be something her father and I can do."

"You can try contacting her. If that doesn't work, I

can locate the names of some reliable deprogrammers who might be able to help." I set aside my tea and pushed to my feet, which were once again comfortably ensconced in sneakers. "For now, at least, my work for you is finished."

"Please, there's one more thing." She was the picture of wild-eyed desperation.

"What's that?"

"I want you to tell Garth."

I thought of the postponed wedding plans and the now-empty honeymoon account. "He'll take the news better if it comes from you."

Besides, a dentist's wife couldn't afford what I'd charge to carry that message.

At 11:00 p.m., I kissed Bill good-night and locked my condo door behind him. After leaving the Langston house, I'd picked up Roger at the office where he'd spent the day with Darcy, and met Bill at my place. He'd brought takeout from the Thirsty Marlin, and I'd filled him in on my findings at Grove Spirit House while we'd eaten. Then we'd taken Roger for a long walk along the waterfront park on the west side of Edgewater Drive.

I was climbing the stairs to bed when the doorbell rang. Roger barked and raced to the front door. I wondered for a second if Bill had forgotten something, but he had a key and could have let himself in. Back downstairs, I turned on the porch light and stared through the peephole at a set of broad shoulders.

"Who is it?"

A deep voice sounded through the closed door. "Garrett Keating with the sheriff's office. I need to talk to you."

A wallet-size folder with a detective's badge and ID appeared in front of the peephole.

I scooped up Roger and opened the door.

"Margaret Skerritt?" he asked.

"Yes?"

"I just have a few routine questions. Okay if I come in?"

I'd been a detective too many years and had used that same line too often to believe Keating's visit was just routine. From the tone of his voice and the grim set of his face, I knew without doubt someone somewhere was in trouble.

I hoped it wasn't me.

CHAPTER 7

I stood aside and Keating stepped in. To his credit, he patted Roger's head.

"Nice dog," he said. "I like dogs."

A tall man, whose polo shirt exhibited well-developed muscles in all the right places, Keating with his dark hair, gray eyes and square jaw had the right combination of male attributes to make any woman's hormones sit up and take notice. He even smelled good. But he was also at least ten years my junior—and, more important, he wasn't Bill.

"Let me put Roger in his crate in the kitchen." I motioned down the hall toward the living room. "Go on in."

Wondering why the Pinellas County Sheriff's Office had sent a detective to my place so late at night, I stowed Roger in his kennel and met Keating in the living room.

"You're working late," I said.

He nodded. "You know how it is."

With hundreds of cases that had kept me up nights, I knew exactly how it was—and it wasn't good. A dire possibility hit me out of the blue, and the blood rushed from my head. In a wave of dizziness, I groped for a chair and sank into it.

"You okay?" Keating's voice seemed to come from far away.

I struggled to speak past the fear that closed my throat. "Tell me you're not here about Bill, that he's okay."

"Bill?"

"Bill Malcolm. He just left a while ago. There hasn't been an accident?"

Strong hands shoved my head toward the floor. "Breathe deep. I'm not here about anyone named Bill."

The dizziness passed, and I sat upright, flushed with relief and feeling incredibly stupid, since I should have known, if I hadn't panicked, that detectives didn't make those kinds of calls. If Bill had been hurt in an accident, a uniformed deputy, not a detective, would have knocked at my door.

"Sorry," I said. "You caught me by surprise. I was afraid—" My ramblings were only making me look sillier. "Why *are* you here?"

Keating folded his muscular frame into a chair across from me and was watching me like a fox eyes a chicken. "Like I said, routine questions."

"There's no such thing. What's going on?"

"Are you willing to tell me everything you did today? Everywhere you went?"

"Any reason I shouldn't? Should I have a lawyer?"

His body was relaxed but his eyes remained alert. "Did you do something that makes you think you need a lawyer?"

How many times had I speared a suspect with that barb? I did a mental review of my day. The only thing I'd done that hinted of impropriety was to impersonate my mother. Surely I couldn't be thrown into the slammer for that, unless my mother had pressed charges. And even *my* mother wouldn't go that far. But only because she wouldn't want the bad press.

I relaxed and sat back in my chair. "My conscience is clean. What do you want to know?"

"Where were you this morning?"

"Grove Spirit House at the end of Hidden Lake Road."

His laser gaze didn't flicker and made me feel like a bug skewered on a pin. I wondered how often I'd produced that same effect in people I'd interrogated. I didn't like being hoisted on my own petard.

"What were you doing there?" Keating asked.

"I'm a private investigator. I was hired by a client to locate her missing daughter. I found her at Grove Spirit House."

"Who was she?"

"Why do you want to know?" I considered the ethics of the situation and whether my answering would violate codes of confidentiality.

Keating sighed. "Look, I know you were a detective. Hell, you're probably better at this than I am, so let's quit beating around the bush. Tell me about Alicia Langston. What did you see at Grove House?"

"Has someone filed a complaint against that creep?"

"Who?"

"The Teacher. I don't know his real name."

Keating grimaced. "Yeah, someone complained."

Probably Jeanette Langston. "About damned time. The guy is lower than pond scum."

"Tell me about your visit."

If I could help nail a con artist, I was happy to talk. I told Keating what Julianne Pritchard had told me and how I'd gone to Grove Spirit House to find Alicia.

"And you found her?"

I nodded. "She was working in the kitchen."

"Doing what?"

I thought back to my brief encounter. "Besides salivating over her mentor? She was rinsing peas in a colander."

He scribbled in a small notebook he'd pulled from his shirt pocket. "Did you see anyone else?"

"Only Celeste, The Teacher's assistant. He told me Celeste and Alicia were the only people there, but he's expecting a group Friday for a weekend retreat."

"Any sign of tension between Alicia and this teacher?"

"Nothing, other than obvious sexual tension on her part. She appeared about as smitten as they come. But he hardly noticed her, except to warn me that she was under a vow of silence."

Keating raised his eyebrows. "A punishment?"

"No, apparently part of the initiation into communing with the Universal Spirit. His words, not mine."

"And Celeste? Any tension between her and the others?"

"She disappeared after greeting me at the main pavilion. I didn't see her again."

He flipped his notebook closed, stowed it in his pocket and rose to his feet. "Thanks, Ms. Skerritt. You've been very helpful."

"Do you have grounds to charge this teacher?"

"Charge him?"

"He's obviously working a con, but since he's operating under the guise of religion, I can't think of any law that he's breaking. You can't arrest someone for simple greed."

Keating's handsome face darkened. "I won't be arresting The Teacher."

"That's too bad. But if you're not investigating his scam, what's this about?"

He paused, as if reluctant to continue. "The Teacher, aka Willard Ashton, died this afternoon."

I blinked in surprise. "But not from natural causes or you wouldn't be here."

Keating nodded.

"Have you made an arrest?"

"I can't—" He glanced at his watch. "What the hell. You'll read it in the morning papers anyway. We arrested Alicia Langston. And, after what you and Celeste have told me, it's a slam-dunk case."

* * *

The next morning I sat in my office, reading the *Tribune*'s account of Willard Ashton's murder and Alicia's arrest, while Bill, ensconced on the sofa with Roger snuggled tightly against him, perused the *Times*.

Frustrated, I folded the paper and tossed it on to my desk. "Nothing else in here besides what Keating already told me."

Bill set his paper aside. "No more here either. We don't even know how Ashton died."

"I tried pumping Keating last night, but he refused to share. Can't blame him. I'd have done the same if it had been my case. He could have called Alicia merely a person of interest but instead implied it's an open-and-shut investigation. He's convinced Alicia's guilty."

Bill raised his eyebrows. "And you're not?"

I shook my head. "Nothing fits. Garth insisted his fiancée is compassionate, spiritual. Julianne claimed her friend was mesmerized by Ashton, which tracks with what I observed. If Alicia was the killer, there had to be some extenuating circumstance."

"Mental instability?" Bill rose to his feet, and Roger hopped off the sofa.

"If you count crazy in love."

"There's a fine line between love and hate, especially when passions run high."

My frustration increased. "We can't even make an educated guess without the facts of the case."

"And Keating's not talking," Bill said with a shrug.

On the bookcase where he was now observing morning traffic, Roger perked up his ears at the ringing of a phone in the reception area.

"And," I scratched at the mild hives that had risen on my forearms, my usual reaction to homicide, "we'll not know those facts until trial, since it's not our case."

Darcy popped her head in the door. "It is now."

Darcy had an uncanny ability to hear all conversations, even through a closed door. If I hadn't known better, I'd have suspected she'd bugged my office.

"Alicia Langston's defense attorney is on the phone," Darcy said. "Teresa Pender, line one."

Darcy returned to her desk, and I shot Bill a questioning look. "Should we take it?"

"The phone call?"

"Alicia's case."

"Why don't you hear what Pender has to say?"

I picked up the phone. "Maggie Skerritt here. What's up, Terry?"

The scrappy little attorney had been defending criminals with all the tenacity of a terrier for as long as I'd been arresting them. On several occasions, I'd endured her hard-hitting cross-examinations on the witness stand. We'd never been friends, but I respected the lawyer. She had ethics, more than I could say for too many others who practiced her specialty of the law.

"Have you read about Alicia Langston's arrest?" Terry asked.

"Not only that, Detective Keating paid me a visit last night."

"Makes sense. Mrs. Langston told me you'd gone to Grove Spirit House yesterday. There's more to this case than meets the eye. Either the cops haven't found it or they're not talking. I need an investigator."

"And your client's innocent, of course?"

Terry surprised me by saying, "I don't want to prejudice you. Ask her yourself."

"When?"

"She's being arraigned this morning. I'll take you to visit her this afternoon. Meet me at the jail at three?"

"As long as one thing's clear," I said.

"What's that?"

"If our agency investigates, we share all our findings with the police, even if they implicate Alicia."

"Once a cop, always a cop, eh, Maggie?"

"So they tell me."

"We're on the same side here," Terry said. "We're both looking for the truth."

With any other defense attorney, I'd have laughed at the claim, but Terry was a cut above the rest. She meant what she said.

"See you at three," I said and hung up.

"So we're taking the case?" Bill asked.

"I'll let you know after I've talked to Alicia."

Bill headed for the door.

"More background checks?" I asked.

He turned. "Yeah, but not for the Historical Society. Just out of curiosity, I'll see what I can find out about Willard Ashton. He's probably scammed plenty of people who'd want him dead. And I'll also try to get a look at the crime scene."

"But we haven't decided to work for Terry yet."

He pointed to the splotches on my forearms.

"When murder gives you hives, I figure we're in this till the case is solved and the spots disappear."

Bill blew me a kiss and left.

Darcy buzzed me on the intercom. "Your mother's on line two."

"Did you tell her I was here?"

"I said I'd check. You want me to tell her you're out?"

I was tempted but resisted. "That excuse is wearing thin. I have to talk to her sometime. I might as well get it over with."

I'd been avoiding Mother's calls for days. She never contacted me unless she either wanted something or had orders to give. She was anxious to finalize her plans for my elaborate wedding, and I'd hoped by putting her off that she'd be too late to make the appropriate arrangements and would finally cease and desist.

But she was my mother, she had been seriously ill, and she was now pushing her eighty-third birthday. Guilt prompted me to pick up the phone and face the consequences.

"Good morning, Mother. How are you?"

I don't know why I bothered to ask. Mother, who always exhibited a strange reluctance to discuss her health, would reply that she was fine. To determine the true state of her well-being, I'd have to ask Caroline, who would then ask Estelle, who had been Mother's live-in housekeeper since I was a child.

"I'm perfectly fine," Mother responded according to her usual script, "but I was beginning to worry that you'd fallen off the face of the earth, Margaret. It's a relief to know you're alive and well." Mother cloaked her sarcasm in such a soft, sweet tone, it took a few seconds to realize I'd been zinged.

"Business is booming."

"Not too booming for you to have lunch with your mother today, I hope?"

When she referred to herself in the third person, I knew I was in trouble, so I bit the bullet. I could always use my meeting with Terry Pender as an excuse for a quick getaway. "Of course not, Mother. Shall I meet you at the club?"

The Yacht Club, bastion of Pelican Bay's rich and famous, was Mother's favorite hangout, but I always felt awkward and out of place in the elegant and exclusive surroundings.

"No, Estelle is preparing lunch here."

I should have felt relieved, but I didn't. I didn't have to be prescient to know that Mother had an agenda.

"Just the two of us?" If Caroline wasn't coming as backup, maybe I could persuade Mother to give up her scheme for my fancy nuptials.

"There's someone at the door," Mother replied. "I'll see you at noon."

With a feeling of foreboding, I hung up the phone. I feared the wedding-planning trap had been sprung.

CHAPTER 8

I arrived at Mother's fifteen minutes early, so I circled the Mediterranean-style waterfront mansion, designed by Misner in the 1920s, and knocked on the kitchen door.

Estelle greeted me with an enthusiastic hug. "Where you been, Miss Margaret? I haven't laid eyes on you in a month of Sundays."

Her white summer uniform was a contrast to her ebony skin but a perfect match for her snowy hair. The last time I'd visited, I'd encouraged her to retire, but Estelle had been horrified at the suggestion. She considered the Skerritts her family, and, in all the ways that mattered, we were.

I perched on a stool beside the counter while Estelle washed romaine in the deep farmhouse sink. The kitchen, with its white cabinets, tall windows and black-and-white tile floor, was the only room in the house where I'd grown up that I truly felt at home. I'd spent more time here with Estelle than I'd ever shared with my socialite mother. Priscilla had always been consumed with committees and charity work, and Daddy had spent long hours at his office and the hospital. With Caroline mortified to be seen with her bratty younger sister, Estelle had been the one constant companion of my youth.

"How's your Mr. Malcolm?" Estelle asked. "I hear you two bought a house."

"We have. Call me on your next afternoon off and I'll take you to see it."

I'd enjoy showing our place to Estelle, who would be genuinely pleased for us and lavish much praise on our simple abode. I had yet to suggest a tour for Mother. I feared if she followed her usual pattern, she'd find fault with everything from the neighborhood to the lack of square footage to the decor, casting a pall on my happiness with our choice.

I gave myself a mental shake and a sharp reminder. Mother's issues were rooted in the disappointments and insecurities of the early years of her marriage and had nothing to do with me, except that I made a handy target. I was trying to learn not to take her attitude personally.

"How many for lunch?" I asked

"Miz Skerritt told me to prepare for four."

"Caroline coming?"

Estelle nodded and arranged romaine leaves on crystal salad plates.

"Who else?"

"Don't know her name, but Miz Skerritt says she's coming all the way from New York City. Miss Caroline is picking the lady up at the airport."

Hope surged. If the guest was one of Mother's old college friends or someone she'd met while working on her multitude of charities, I was off the hook. My very proper mother wouldn't discuss family business in front of a guest.

"Can I give you a hand, Estelle?"

"Shoo, child. I can handle this. You go on in and see your mama. I know she's been missing you."

I didn't correct Estelle's delusion but braced myself and left the kitchen by way of the butler's pantry. I passed through the dining room, and the front door opened. Caroline stepped in and stood aside for the woman from New York to enter.

One glance at the haute couture of my sister and her companion convinced me that I, in my white cropped pants, leaf-green pullover and matching flip-flops, appropriate for almost any other venue in Pelican Bay, was seriously underdressed.

Mother, also dressed and coiffed suitably to have tea with the Queen, entered the hall from the central courtyard. "Madame Lapierre, how kind of you to come."

"I am honored to be invited," the woman replied, her speech lightly peppered with accents of her French origins. "The drive across the bay on the causeway was *magnifique*."

"You know Caroline, of course," Mother said, then caught sight of me. Her face fell as she took in my apparel. "And this is my younger daughter, Margaret."

"Ah," Madame Lapierre said, "so this is the bride-to-be?"

"Actually," I said with a smile, "I prefer to think of myself as a private investigator."

Mother grimaced as if I'd just announced I was bisexual, but Madame Lapierre seemed impressed.

"You must have many stories to tell, no?"

"If ethics allowed," I said.

"*Moi, aussi.* I have many stories, but a loose tongue would destroy my business."

With a sense of impending doom, I asked, "What business are you in?"

Caroline gripped my elbow as if afraid I'd cut and run. "Madame Lapierre is New York's premier wedding planner."

I gritted my teeth and forced a smile. "How nice. And you're here on vacation?"

"*Mais non.*" She appeared momentarily confused, then assumed a hopeful expression. "Your *maman* must have arranged my arrival as a surprise. I am here to plan your wedding."

I shot Mother a tight smile, more like a grimace. "Well, it worked. I'm definitely surprised."

Estelle appeared in the doorway to the dining room. "Luncheon is served, Miz Skerritt."

Mother herded us into the dining room, seated me on her left and Madame Lapierre on her right. Caroline took a chair opposite Mother at the end of the antique refectory table that had once graced a Spanish monastery.

Estelle served a Waldorf salad, baked fillets of mahi-mahi and a medley of summer vegetables, all prepared in her inimitable delicious style, but I couldn't eat. I was too busy trying to figure how to thwart Mother's plans without making her look bad in front of her guest, an unpardonable sin.

"So, Margaret," Madame said. "What kind of wedding do you want?"

"Small and uncomplicated."

"Vraiment?" Madame turned a puzzled gaze on Mother, who was busy glaring at me.

"Margaret's such a kidder," Caroline said with a nervous laugh and a pointed stare in my direction. "Mother's planning on eight hundred guests. That's not exactly small."

"Or uncomplicated," I added.

Madame's eyes met mine across the table. Her dark eyebrows arched above her questioning eyes. I threw her a helpless look. She seemed to register my reluctance because the gaze she returned was sympathetic. Rather than raise Mother's ire by dragging my feet further, I concentrated on cutting my mahimahi into cubes of equal size and allowed the conversation to flow around me. I'd ask for Madame's card before I left, on the pretext of refining details, then call to tell her I wouldn't be going through with Mother's plans.

Mother would lose her deposit and Madame's travel expenses, which was bad enough, but better in her book than losing face in front of a guest.

When Estelle served the crème brûlée, I excused myself. "I have a meeting scheduled with a client. I'm sure Madame understands how that is."

The Frenchwoman's commiserating nod implied that she understood the subtext of what I was saying, and, despite the disapproving clucks and frowns of Mother and Caroline, I made my escape.

I killed time by taking Roger for a walk and returning him to Darcy at the office before I met Terry Pender in Largo outside the entrance to the county jail.

Once inside, after a search of Terry's briefcase and my purse and the surrender of my weapon, we were admitted to a small, windowless room, furnished only with a metal table bolted to the floor and two chairs.

Terry, wearing a brilliant red power suit, paced the cell. At only five feet tall, less than a hundred pounds, and with her blond hair close-cropped in a waifish Peter Pan cut, she looked as if a puff of wind could carry her away. Many a prosecutor had been lulled into complacency by her nonthreatening demeanor and had lived to regret it. Having seen Ms. Pender in action in the courtroom, I knew that bright red suit packaged the full explosive power of C-4.

"The judge denied bail at this morning's arraignment," Terry said, "as expected. But I'm worried about this kid. Alicia's fragile and cerebral. She'll be eaten alive in this place."

"What do you want me to do?" I asked.

"Interrogate her as you would any suspect," Terry said.

"That can get rough."

Terry sighed. "She'll have to learn to handle rough before all this is over."

"Especially if she's convicted."

"Bite your tongue, Maggie. I don't intend to lose this case."

A key turned in the lock, the steel door swung open, and Alicia stepped into the room. She looked so different from the girl I'd seen yesterday that I took a moment to recognize her. Her face was swollen and splotched from crying, her long hair wild and tangled, and her willowy figure engulfed by pants and a blouse that, except for their bright orange color, resembled hospital scrubs.

A guard removed her handcuffs, and Terry, with

amazing gentleness, led Alicia to the table and one of the metal chairs. Terry motioned me to take the chair across from Alicia.

"This is Maggie Skerritt, a private investigator," the attorney informed her client. "She's here to help you and has some questions. I want you to tell her everything."

Alicia nodded, but the girl appeared so wounded, I wondered how much she actually comprehended.

Terry retreated to a corner, leaned against the wall and folded her arms across her chest.

"Tell me what happened yesterday," I said to Alicia.

She lifted her head at the sound of my voice and studied my face with a frown. "Do I know you?"

"I was at Grove Spirit House yesterday morning."

Comprehension flitted across her tear-stained features. "You look different."

"So do you."

Her lips lifted slightly in a rueful smile. "Are you going to help me?"

"That depends."

"On what?"

"On whether you killed Willard Ashton."

Fresh tears trickled down her cheeks and her shoulders shook with a sob. "The Teacher? Why would I kill him? He was wonderful."

"He was very good at what he did," I hedged. "Now tell me about yesterday."

"Everything seems like such a blur."

"Take your time, but don't leave out anything. Even the smallest details can be very important."

"You're going to get me out of here, aren't you?" Her tone was pleading, desperate.

"You'll have to stand trial first," I said. "If Terry can prove your innocence, you'll be released. But for her to defend you, we need to know everything. Let's start with yesterday."

Alicia took a deep breath, wiped her nose with the back of her hand and nodded. "It was almost exactly like every day I'd spent there."

"You had a routine?"

"The Teacher said I needed discipline in order to join with the Universal Spirit."

I nodded and waited.

"Yesterday," she continued, "I got up at daybreak—"

"Where did you sleep?"

"In one of the tiki huts by the lake. It was scary at first with no walls and all those bugs, but I was getting used to it. The Teacher said I had to learn to shut out this world—"

"To commune with the Universal Spirit." I couldn't keep the sarcasm from my voice, but Alicia didn't seem to notice.

"After bathing in the lake, I did my morning meditation in the gazebo. Celeste sounded the gong at ten, the signal for me to begin my chores. I went straight to the kitchen. I was preparing the midday meal when you came in."

"And after that?"

"I served The Teacher in the dining room and returned to my hut for my afternoon studies. Not long after that, I heard Celeste's screams, coming from the dining pavilion. I ran as fast as I could. The Teacher was on the floor, unconscious." Alicia started crying again.

Neither Detective Keating nor the news reports had given cause of death. "How did he die?"

"I thought he'd taken ill. He'd thrown up, and his skin was covered with a red rash. Celeste called 911, and we waited outside for the paramedics." She shook her head sadly. "There wasn't anything they could do. He was already…gone."

"What did the paramedics tell you?"

"They called the police and the medical examiner and told Celeste and me to stay out of the dining pavilion. A sheriff's deputy stayed with us. After the medical examiner left with…the body, a detective came over and asked who'd prepared the meal. I told him I had. He asked if Celeste had helped."

"Had she?"

Alicia shook her head. "Celeste stayed out of the kitchen. I even unloaded the groceries from her car and put them away after she went shopping. Her job was to take care of all the paperwork, reservations for retreats and bookkeeping." Alicia shook her head. "When I told that to the detective, he arrested me."

"Doc Cline claims Ashton was poisoned," Terry interjected from her corner.

"That can't be," Alicia insisted, "unless he had some kind of allergy. He'd eaten that same recipe before and liked it. That's why I fixed it again."

Doc Cline, the medical examiner, was good at her job. If she said Ashton had been poisoned, the guy had been poisoned. If I knew how, I'd have a better idea what the hell had happened.

"Did you eat any of the dish you'd prepared?" I asked.

"I'd been fasting ever since I entered Grove Spirit House. I was allowed only fruit juice in the mornings and evenings."

"Tell me about this meal you fixed."

"It was a pea, pesto and penne pasta salad." Meeting my gaze, she answered without hesitation. If the kid was guilty, she was doing a first-class job of covering herself. She either had a clear conscience or, as with too many I'd encountered in my line of work, no conscience at all.

"Could anyone have tampered with the ingredients?" I asked.

Alicia thought for a moment. "I opened a fresh box of whole-grain pasta, a new bottle of olive oil for the pesto. But the packages that contained the basil for the pesto and the peas had been opened and replaced in the refrigerator when I made the salad two days earlier."

"So someone could have tampered with them?"

"I guess. But who? I never saw Celeste enter the kitchen. The only other person around was Hector Morales, the lawn guy, but that was almost a week ago, the first day I was there."

Remembering The Teacher's overt sexuality, I took a stab in the dark. "Did Ashton ever come on to you?"

Alicia blushed and lowered her eyes. "He held me. But it's not what you think. He said our closeness represented our oneness—"

"With the Universal Spirit." Ashton had been a self-serving creep, but that wasn't a capital offense. Someone, however, must have thought so. And my gut was telling me it wasn't Alicia.

"Any other questions?" Terry asked.

I shook my head. "Not for now."

"Anything you need?" the attorney asked Alicia.

Alicia, eyes wide with fright, looked about ten years old. "Just to go home."

The guard reappeared to take her to her cell and Terry and I left behind her. I retrieved my gun, walked with Terry into the parking lot and stopped beside her car, a gigantic Expedition that made the attorney look like a pygmy.

"What do you think?" she asked.

"I don't believe Alicia did it," I said. "At the moment, however, I have nothing to base that on but twenty-three years' experience and an instinct that's been right most of the time."

"The kid lacks motive," Terry agreed. "She obviously adored Ashton. His death has traumatized her as much as being arrested. Will you take the case?"

I nodded grimly. "Alicia's going to need all the help she can get."

CHAPTER 9

Bill handed me the beer he'd poured into a frosted pilsner and sat beside me on the deck to watch the sunset. Mouthwatering aromas had emanated from the galley when he'd opened the cabin's sliding glass door, but between lunch with Mother and my jailhouse visit with Alicia Langston, my appetite was on hiatus.

Bill must have noticed my somber demeanor.

"Your mother and Caroline still on your back?" he asked.

I took a long drink and shuddered. "It gets worse every day."

"What's worse than eight hundred wedding guests?"

"Eight bridesmaids."

He grinned. "What's next, ten lords a-leaping?"

I swatted him on the arm. "You won't think this is so funny come Valentine's Day when they have you gussied up in a tux with tails, looking like an overgrown penguin on display to a crowd of strangers."

He struggled to straighten his face. "No offense, Margaret, but do you *know* eight women well enough to have them serve as wedding attendants?"

"I don't have to. Caroline and Mother have it all figured out. Caroline will be matron of honor. And Mother plans to ask the daughters of eight of *her* friends, girls I knew in high school, to be bridesmaids. Mother will probably select your groomsmen, too."

"Priscilla is nothing if not resourceful," Bill said with a touch of admiration.

"That's not the half of it," I said with a sigh. "They've reserved the sanctuary of the Presbyterian church, hoping it will be large enough, since it seats a thousand. That will include the riffraff who won't be invited to dinner. The reception will be held on the lawn at Mother's, with the ballroom of the Pelican Beach Hilton booked in case of rain."

"Sounds like all the bases are covered."

I chugged beer, hoping for oblivion. "You should have heard them oohing and aahing with Madame Lapierre over details. They decided the bridesmaids' dresses will be plum, for Pete's sake, and their bouquets those god-awful purple orchids. I *hate* orchids."

"Moot point, isn't it?"

"What?"

He took my hand and threaded his fingers through mine. "Bridesmaids, dresses, flowers. Since you're not going through with the plans, what do any of them matter?"

"I've been letting my mother and sister steamroller me, which proves what a total wimp I am. That's what matters."

Bill threw back his head and laughed. "You, a wimp? I've seen you take down a 250-pound thug, high on crack, with the whack of a baton to the back of his knees. You're no wimp, Margaret."

I felt a glimmer of hope. "You think a baton will work on Mother?"

"How about a simple *no?*"

"My mother doesn't understand simple. And few people dare say *no* to her. But you're right. I have to tell her."

"The longer you put it off, the harder it will be."

I nodded. "But Mother seems so pleased with me

while she's making these plans. I hate to cause her to revert to her former disapproval. Is that sick, or what?"

"That's human. We all want our parents to approve of us."

Shamed by my obsession with petty problems in light of Bill's recent loss, I squeezed his hand. "I know you miss your dad."

Bill's father had died from complications of Alzheimer's last month, and his death had hit Bill hard. He'd had a terrible enough time handling his dad's death, but he was also racked with guilt over his sense of relief. Watching the big man, who'd been hale and hearty all his life, deteriorate both mentally and physically had torn Bill apart. He'd both welcomed his father's death and been devastated by it.

"I miss Dad," Bill said, "but I'd already lost him months ago. He hadn't recognized me in over a year." He seemed to shake off his sadness.

I'd never known Bill to remain unhappy for long. His ubiquitous optimism and joy in living were two of the many traits I loved about him.

A boat entered the row of slips where Bill's cabin cruiser was docked, and its wake stirred the waters, gently rocking the deck where we sat. The music of the Fifth Dimension drifted across the marina from an oldies radio station, playing on a nearby sailboat. Seagulls flocked overhead as charter boats at the far side of the marina unloaded their passengers and catches of the day. The scene was calm, peaceful, but my insides were tied in knots by events I'd allowed to rocket out of control.

"So," Bill said in his practical way, "what are you going to do about these grandiose wedding plans?"

"I did call Madame Lapierre's New York office this afternoon and left a message on her voice mail to warn her that I would not be participating in Mother's big fat wedding."

"Good. That's a start."

I sighed. "And I'm still working up the courage to break the news to Mother in a way she'll understand and accept."

"You always rise to the challenge, Margaret," he said with such confidence I was beginning to believe I could actually confront Mother without her disowning me, which she'd done once before, when I'd had to arrest the daughter of her best friend.

"I'm beginning to think George Burns was right," I said.

"The comic?"

"Yeah, he claimed happiness was having a large, loving, close-knit family—living in another city."

Bill laughed. "As long as you keep your sense of humor, you'll be okay. Now, want to hear about my afternoon?"

I was glad to change the subject. "Any luck on Ashton?"

"Nothing. It's as if the man didn't exist before he showed up in Pelican Bay."

"That's a red flag right there. If he changed his identity, he's either running from the law or someone who had it in for him. Or both."

"My thoughts precisely. That's why I've enlisted Adler's help."

My former partner now worked as a detective for the Clearwater PD. Young enough to be my son, he'd always stirred my maternal instincts. They came to his defense now. "Isn't he awfully busy with his own caseload?"

"Not to worry." Bill patted my hand. "He's simply going to run Ashton's name through his databases and see if he gets a hit. Keating's probably already done that, but I doubt he'll be sharing anything until the rules of discovery require it."

"I'll try talking to Keating again," I said.

"You think he'll bend?"

"I'll use my feminine wiles."

"Poor guy," Bill said. "He doesn't have a chance."

"Be serious."

"I am serious." He leaned over and kissed me.

I enjoyed kissing him back.

Long minutes later, after I'd come up for air, Bill said, "I went by Grove Spirit House today, but the deputy at the gate wouldn't let me in."

"We need to inspect the crime scene and interview Celeste."

"Terry will have to get us access," he said. "But my trip wasn't wasted. I did a perimeter check."

I recalled the eight-foot chain-link fence and the undergrowth that surrounded it. "Through all those weeds?"

He nodded.

"Find anything besides sandspurs, beggar weed, snakes and fire ants?"

He nodded again. "Someone else had recently trampled the weeds along a section of the fence."

"The sheriff's investigators?"

"I don't think so. There were fresh tire tracks in the sandy soil where a vehicle had pulled off the road, just out of range of the surveillance camera. And I could see through the fence that someone had also beaten a path through the grove toward the retreat compound." He stood. "Wait here. I'll be right back."

He returned a moment later with several digital photos he'd printed out from his computer and handed them to me. Sure enough, someone had recently crushed the weeds between two rows of orange trees. But most interesting of all was a close-up of the top of the fence where the trailblazer had gained entry to the property. Snagged in the exposed ends of the wires was a scrap of fabric, a bright, tasteless plaid that I recognized immediately.

"That material is the same as the shirt Garth Swinburn was wearing when I interviewed him the day before Ashton was murdered."

"You're sure?" Bill asked.

"A fabric that ugly is hard to forget. But when I

spoke with Garth the day before the murder, he swore he didn't know where Alicia was."

"Looks like he found out."

I wasn't pleased with the way this investigation was headed. I didn't want to clear one nice kid just to have another one charged. "We'll have to question Garth again."

"I'll do it in the morning," Bill said. "Want to come along?"

I shook my head. "Two of us might intimidate him, make him clam up."

"Speaking of clam—" Bill said with a glance at his watch.

"As in 'happy as'?"

He kissed the tip of my nose. "As in supper's ready."

Shortly after seven the next morning, I walked into Iris's Restaurant in Dunedin and searched the already crowded room for a familiar face. I found her, tucked in a corner at a booth by the window, reading the *Times*.

"Mind if I join you?"

Doc Cline looked up in surprise. "Maggie! What are you doing here?"

"Having breakfast," I hedged.

No need to admit that I'd already called her office and home with no results. Doc was a creature of habit, and if she wasn't at work or home this time of morning, the next likely spot was the family restaurant near her Dunedin residence, a popular eatery opposite the stadium where the Toronto Blue Jays played their spring-training games.

"Sit," she said.

I scooted across from her, and a waitress appeared at my elbow and filled a mug with coffee.

"It's good to see you," Doc said. "It's been a couple of months, hasn't it?" Her smile faded. "Don't tell me. You're working another murder."

"How can you tell?" I sipped my coffee.

"Besides the hives on your face? Because solving homicides is what you do, isn't it?"

I shrugged. "That—and catch dognappers," I added, remembering how I'd obtained Roger.

The waitress reappeared and placed a huge stack of pancakes, sprinkled with chopped pecans and sliced bananas, in front of Doc. The ME proceeded to smother everything on the plate with maple syrup.

Doc, who was pushing retirement, somehow managed to tuck away such a breakfast and maintain the figure and muscle tone of a young female jock. I envied her metabolism and advised the waitress to bring me whole-grain toast sans butter.

"Tell me about Willard Ashton," I said. "Terry Pender says you've determined that he was poisoned."

"Pender's the defense attorney for that young woman they arrested?"

I nodded.

"And you're working for Pender?"

I nodded again, while Doc wolfed another mouthful of calories and chewed thoughtfully. She washed it down with a swig of coffee and said, "Guess I can tell you what I know. It'll come out in discovery anyway."

"Probably in the news before that." I indicated her copy of the *Times*.

"Ashton was definitely poisoned," Doc said. "The symptoms were clear."

"Any guess what kind of poison?"

Her reply was unequivocal. "Belladonna."

The ready answer surprised me, since Doc didn't indulge in casual speculation. "You have the toxicology report already? That usually takes weeks."

She shook her head. "The report's not back, but I

know because Mick Rafferty at the crime lab found belladonna in the remains of Ashton's meal."

"Someone spiked his food?" Things weren't looking good for the home team, since Alicia had already admitted to being the only person who worked in the kitchen and to serving Ashton's lunch.

"It's more complex than that," Doc said. "Crime-scene techs also found belladonna in the refrigerator."

"Why would the murderer keep poison in plain sight, especially if they'd just killed someone?"

"It wasn't exactly in plain sight." Doc had worked her way through half her stack of pancakes. I nibbled dry toast that tasted like sawdust. "Belladonna leaves were mixed in with a bag of fresh basil in the crisper and belladonna berries scattered among peas in a package in the freezer."

I sighed. "No point then in questioning pharmaceutical companies about who purchased the poison."

"You'd be like a dog chasing its tail. Belladonna, aka deadly nightshade, is a common weed in this area. Most people have it growing somewhere in their yards, along fences or under trees or shrubs where birds sit and deposit the seeds in their droppings."

"If having the means to murder covers everyone

with access to the weeds," I said with sinking expectations, "looks like I'd better concentrate on motive and opportunity."

"I'm glad I don't have your job," Doc said with obvious sympathy. "Clearing Ms. Langston is going to be tough under the circumstances."

"To each his own." I'd take detective work over performing autopsies any day. "By the way, has anyone stepped forward to claim the body?"

"Yeah, Ashton's wife."

"His wife?"

"She came into the office late yesterday to ask when his remains would be released."

"She give a name?"

"Just Mrs. Ashton."

"What did she look like?"

"Tall, slender, long dark hair held back by a headband and wearing a tie-dyed granny dress and sandals. We'd have called her a flower child, back in my day."

Celeste, the sultry-voiced receptionist, was married to The Teacher? Now that was an interesting turn of events.

"Thanks, Doc."

"Good to see you, Maggie. We never got to do that

lunch," she said with a grin, referring to our standing joke, "but at least we've done breakfast."

"Sounds like a line from *Casablanca*."

I paid my bill and hurried to the car. I reached for the manila envelope on the front seat and pulled out the photos Bill had given me. In a close-up of the trampled grass on the other side of the fence where Bill had found the scrap of plaid, tall weeds with dull green leaves, bell-shaped flowers and unripe berries that looked like garden peas grew in abundance. I studied the other pictures.

The entire grove was thick with deadly nightshade.

CHAPTER 10

I left Iris's and drove south on Douglas Avenue to Pelican Bay, then west on Main to downtown and the sheriff's office substation that had once been the Pelican Bay Police Department.

Entering the familiar doors created a momentary disorientation and an overwhelming sadness, as if I were visiting a home where I'd lived for years, only to find a new family and their furnishings had taken residence and destroyed all traces of my ever having been there. The old PD had been my family, and now its former members were gone with the wind: Adler and Rudy Beaton to work for the Clearwater PD, Steve Johnson clerking at Home Depot, and Darcy at Pelican Bay Investigations. Chief Shelton had retired, and Lenny Jacobs and the others had found employment in various parts of the state. Several had abandoned law enforcement for less stressful careers. Like children of divorce, we'd never be a true family again. That reality made my heart ache.

I stopped at the reception desk, once Darcy's domain as dispatcher, and asked to see Detective Keating. The deputy on duty directed me down the hall, ironically to the same cubicle that had been my former office.

Keating was seated behind what I couldn't help thinking of as *my* desk, but shot to his feet when he saw me in the doorway and greeted me with a toothy grin.

"Margaret Skerritt! What a pleasant surprise. Come in. Have a seat."

With morning sunlight streaming through the window and illuminating Keating like a klieg light, he looked like Tom Selleck in his younger days as Magnum, P.I., but with his hair trimmed and minus the mustache, shorts and Hawaiian shirt. Keating wore instead khaki slacks and a fitted dark green knit shirt with the sheriff's office logo above the breast pocket.

"Do you have a minute?" I asked.

"For you, I have all the time in the world." He hurried around the desk and made a show of grabbing me a chair from Adler's desk. Correction, what used to be Adler's desk.

Keating was actually flirting with me, which made me instantly suspicious and wonder if he knew I was working for Pender and was hoping to sweet talk me out of any facts of the case he wasn't aware of.

I settled in Adler's chair, but instead of returning to his seat, Keating propped a hip on the desk in front of me, too close for comfort, and continued to beam at me as if I were a long-awaited Christmas present, finally arrived.

I wasn't there to play games so went straight to the point. "I need access to the crime scene."

He frowned and looked confused, as if I'd spoken in a language he hadn't understood.

"The Willard Ashton murder," I added. "I'm working for Terry Pender, who's defending Alicia Langston."

His expression sobered. "I wondered who'd take her case."

"You didn't know?"

He shook his head and appeared honestly surprised, which blew my theory on the reason for his flirtation out of the water.

"Pender's got her work cut out for her," Keating said. "Langston prepared the meal that killed Ashton. Her prints are not only all over the serving dish but also on the packages of ingredients from the refrigerator where the poison was found."

"Belladonna," I said.

Now he really looked surprised. "I'd heard you were good. You don't waste any time do you?"

Except right now, conversing with a guy who wouldn't give me a straight answer. "Has the crime-scene unit released the scene?"

"They finished up last night. Want me to drive you out there?" His question held all the eagerness of an enthusiastic puppy dog.

"Thanks, but I prefer to do my own investigation. Conflict of interest. You know how it is."

He nodded, serious for an instant, then his wide smile returned. "Then I'll just have to think of another reason for us to get together."

If he thought coming on to me would deter my investigation, he was in for a shock.

"No need." I pushed to my feet and headed for the door to avoid the signals Keating was emanating, like a guy who'd been on a desert island for years and I was the first female he'd encountered upon reaching civilization. "I'm sure I'll see you in court."

His face mirrored his disappointment. "But that could be months."

"I hope so," I said. "I have a lot of work to do before then."

With a wave over my shoulder, I hurried from his cubicle and headed for my car.

My office was only a few minutes away, and Bill was waiting when I arrived. I briefed him on what I'd learned from Doc Cline and told him we had permission from Keating to visit Grove Spirit House.

"If Celeste will let us in," Bill said.

"We could always go over the fence like Garth did." I'd climbed many a fence in my patrol days and hoped I hadn't lost the touch. Or, more importantly, the muscle tone. "Did you talk to him?"

I sank onto the sofa beside Bill and looked for Roger before remembering I'd left him at home this morning when I'd headed out for an early meeting with the ME. The little bugger had wormed his way into my heart so thoroughly, I missed him when he wasn't around.

"Garth admits he was at Grove Spirit House the night before Ashton died," Bill said. "Even showed me the shirt he tore when he went over the fence."

"Going in?"

"Coming out. He was in a hurry, but I'll get to that."

"What was he doing there?"

"After you talked to Julianne Pritchard that night, her conscience was bothering her, so she called Garth and spilled the beans. She wanted him to check on Alicia right away to see if she was really okay. You must have put the fear in her," he added with a look of admiration.

"Only way I could make her talk."

"Worked well. She told Garth everything she'd told you."

"Even about the emptied honeymoon account?"

Bill nodded.

"So Garth could have been truly worried, as he said, or he could have been royally pissed off. Could you tell?"

"He was agitated when I spoke with him," Bill said, "but who wouldn't be if his fiancée has been arrested for murder?"

"So after Julianne told him where to find Alicia, Garth took off?"

Bill nodded. "He drove straight to Grove Spirit House, but claims no one would let him in the gate."

"So he decided to go over the fence."

"Not until he saw the truck pulled alongside it out of range of the security camera."

"Those tire tracks you photographed weren't Garth's?"

Bill shook his head. "Garth left his car in the driveway entrance. He says the other vehicle was an older model Chevy pickup with a Florida tag."

"Did he get the number?"

"Just noted that it was one of those specialty tags. Said it had fish or something aquatic on it."

"He saw that in the dark?" I was beginning to doubt Garth's story.

"He claims he'd taken a flashlight from his car. When he saw the brush beaten down between the pickup and the fence and a similar path through the grove, he decided to follow it, afraid someone was up to no good and scared for Alicia."

"Do you believe him?" I asked.

"He exhibited none of the usual characteristics of lying or a guilty conscience."

"Could be a sociopath. They're hard to shake."

"You met him," Bill said. "What did you think?"

"Seemed like a guy in love and worried sick about his fiancée."

Bill nodded. "Even more so now. That's why he was so eager to talk. He's hoping what, or rather who he saw will clear Alicia."

"Who did he see?"

"Garth says he got only as far as a building with a fountain on the walkway when he was confronted by a man with a machete. The guy told him to get out or die. And he said it in Spanish."

"So Garth chose to get out," I said, "which explains the snagged shirt on the fence. I hope he got a good look at the other guy first."

Bill pulled a notebook from his shirt pocket and consulted it. "Short, bald, with a scar across his right cheek. Not the kind of guy, Garth said, who would listen to reason."

"And that's it?"

"Garth called 911 on his cell phone when he reached his car. Figured he'd let the sheriff's office handle it, especially since he wasn't armed."

"Did they?"

"Eventually. Must have been a busy night. But, according to Garth, the Hispanic intruder bailed out over the fence a few minutes after Garth did and took off in his truck before the deputies arrived."

"And Garth didn't get the tag number while he waited?"

"Too rattled, he said." Bill frowned. "But here's the oddest part. Garth says that when the deputies arrived, some woman answered the intercom and wouldn't let them in, either. She insisted there was no problem and everyone else in the compound was asleep."

"You think Garth's telling the truth?" I asked.

Bill shrugged.

"If Garth placed the 911 call," I said, "it will be logged in. Another bit of info Keating neglected to share."

"Info that shakes his case." Bill flipped his notebook closed and returned it to his pocket. "Instead of just Ashton's wife and Alicia, we now know there were two others on the premises the night before the murder who might have placed deadly nightshade in the food in the refrigerator."

I considered the possibilities. "That fact might be enough for Terry to plant reasonable doubt in a jury's deliberations."

"But, if we've misjudged Swinburn, this story could be merely a ploy to throw us off track. We have only Garth's word that there *was* an intruder," Bill reminded me.

"Unless we can find him."

"Middle-aged Hispanic in an old pickup? The state's crawling with immigrants. Needle in a haystack."

"I love a challenge," I admitted. "First, we check out Hector Morales, the groundskeeper. If the intruder wasn't him, he may know who it was."

Bill pointed out the envelope of digital pictures I'd brought in from my car. "We have good shots of the tire tracks. Those photos may come in handy if we need to match a vehicle."

"Celeste still tops my list of suspects," I said.

"Because she's the vic's wife?"

"That and the fact that, according to Alicia, Celeste buys the groceries."

"Time to pay her a visit." Bill stood and pulled me from the sofa. In a deft move, he slid his arms around my waist and tugged me against him.

I gave him a fierce hug and broke away. "Better not get sidetracked. We have a case to solve."

"All work and no play—"

I stood on tiptoe and kissed him lightly. "We can play later."

CHAPTER 11

At Grove Spirit House, we were surprised when Celeste responded to our call on the intercom by opening the electronic gate.

Bill drove the SUV down the crushed-shell drive and surveyed the surrounding vegetation.

"Damned shame how these trees have been neglected," he observed.

Bill's father had been a citrus grower all his life, and Bill had inherited a thousand acres of groves when his dad had died. A foreman continued to operate the groves for Bill, who was under constant pressure by developers to sell. The land, near Plant City east of Tampa, was worth millions, but Bill hated to see the trees ripped out and the soil paved over with cheek-by-jowl houses and concrete networks of streets and sidewalks. He, like me and other natives, considered population growth an insidious disease, eating away acre by acre at what was left of Old Florida, destroying groves, wetlands, natural habitats and a way of life that would soon be only a memory.

We didn't consider ourselves in the same league as rabid environmentalists or idealistic tree huggers, but we mourned the loss of the state's rural character that had been an integral part of our youth. We'd grown up with isolated pristine beaches lined with dunes and sea oats instead of condos, and miles of rolling pastures, pine woods and citrus groves. Today's young Floridians experienced primarily high rises, concrete, traffic and Disney World.

The grounds at Grove Spirit House reminded us of what we'd lost. Late-morning sunlight glistened on the calm surface of the lake, ringed by cypress swamps. The trees with their distinctive knees rose from the dark waters and their branches were filled with great white herons and anhingas, wings spread to dry in the sun. A trio of galinules that had somehow avoided becoming gator bait glided among the cattails near the shore. The scene was soothing, peaceful, not the place you'd expect to find murder and mayhem.

Celeste was waiting for us in front of the fountain. She wore black slacks and an embroidered black tunic top, and her feet were bare. Her long dark hair had been plaited into two braids that hung over her shoulders. Her pale face was devoid of makeup and expression.

"We're sorry for your loss, Mrs. Ashton," Bill said gently, "and regret this intrusion on your grief."

"I don't understand why you're here," she replied. "The police said they'd completed their investigation."

Bill repeated our names, which he'd given her at the gate, and explained that we were private investigators. "We've been hired by Ms. Langston's defense counsel. In order for Alicia to receive a fair trial, we need to investigate everything that the police had access to."

"She killed my husband," Celeste said in a strange, uninflected voice. "I'm not inclined to help her in any way."

"If she's guilty, nothing we do will change that," I said.

Celeste scrutinized my face. "You were here the day he died."

I nodded. "I'd been hired by Alicia's parents. She'd gone missing, and they wanted to know whether she was all right."

"You tricked us," Celeste said in the same flat tone.

So far, the woman had shown no emotion of any

kind, apparently in shock over the death of her husband and suffering a blessed numbness that would probably wear off all too soon. Or she was in shock from having killed him. Which one, I'd have to find a way to prove.

"I had to find Alicia," I said, "and you wouldn't let me in."

"It's a private retreat. You had no right." Strong words, but also spoken with no affect, as if her body were a dwelling into which her spirit had retreated and bolted the door. Nothing escaped except the dullness of her words.

"My colleague had the right to reassure frantic parents when their only child had gone missing," Bill said in his most consoling tone. "Mind if I have a look around while she asks you some questions?"

Celeste shrugged. "I have nothing to say and there's nothing to see. And if you're trying to prove that murderer's innocence, then you're wasting your time and mine."

"You want your husband's killer convicted, don't you?" Bill asked in his most reasonable voice.

Celeste nodded.

She was saying the right words, but their lack of any

feeling was giving me the creeps. She wouldn't look us in the eyes, but gazed past our shoulders, her dark brown, almost black eyes appearing slightly unfocused, like a near-sighted person without her glasses or someone high on drugs. With her gaunt pale looks, straight black hair, and dark clothes, she reminded me of Morticia from TV's *Addams Family* or Elvira, but without the curvaceous voluptuousness of the Mistress of the Dark. The woman was full-blown weird, but that didn't make her guilty.

"If the defense team is denied access to the crime scene and other evidence and witnesses," Bill explained, "even if Alicia is found guilty, her conviction could be overturned on appeal. Better to go by the book if you want a verdict that sticks."

For a moment, Celeste said nothing, as if she hadn't heard or understood. She continued to gaze at the lake with unfocused eyes.

"Let's get this over with," she finally agreed. "I have arrangements to make."

I stayed with Celeste, and Bill set off for a tour of the grounds and dining hall. His digital camera dangled from a strap on his shoulder. The CSU had removed whatever evidence they'd found, but, if they'd missed anything, Bill could photograph it. We had no authority to take anything from the scene, unless Celeste gave us permission. She'd already made it clear, however, she'd do nothing to assist Alicia's case.

The June sun was beating down, sucking the moisture from the air into anvil-shaped clouds that promised afternoon thunderstorms. A trickle of sweat slid down my backbone. I pointed to the gazebo by the lake. "Can we talk in the shade?"

Like a sleepwalker, Celeste turned, strode across the yard and climbed the gazebo steps. In the relative coolness of the vine-covered structure, she sat on a built-in bench that circled the balustrade.

I sat beside her, a few feet away. "What makes you so sure that Alicia killed your husband?"

Again, Celeste stared at the lake before turning her dull gaze on me. "The girl was obviously disturbed."

"Insane?"

"Wildly in love."

I couldn't deny her charge. I'd witnessed Alicia's infatuation. "Alicia had only been here a few days. How could she have fallen that deeply in love so quickly?"

"She had only lived at Spirit House a few days. But she spent hours at a time with my husband for weeks before her entry here, while she was working on her dissertation. She called it research. I think she just wanted to be near him."

"But if she loved him, why kill him?"

"Because if she couldn't have him, no one would." Celeste clasped her long fingers in her lap and studied them. "She was trying to kill me, too. I would have died, if I'd been on time for lunch. The salad Alicia prepared had been intended for both of us."

Chilled, in spite of the heat, by Celeste's cold, deadened tone, I waited for her to continue.

"I was leaving our quarters for the dining hall when the phone rang. It was a client canceling his reservation for the retreat this weekend and arguing about a refund. Now the entire retreat is canceled."

"And your husband started lunch without you?"

"He was a man of great appetites."

She'd opened the door, so I stepped through it. "Apparently his appetites extended to Alicia Langston. According to her, he embraced her frequently. That must have bothered you."

She lifted her head, cast her eyes in my direction, but even her body language was devoid of emotion. "He embraced all the novices, men and women alike, a symbolic gesture of their oneness with the Universal Spirit."

"And you were never jealous?"

At last, something flickered in the depths of those strange, almost-black eyes. Anger? Annoyance? Regret? I couldn't tell.

"Never," she said.

"How long had you been married?"

"What does that have to do with Alicia Langston?"

"Did she know you and The Teacher were man and wife?"

Celeste shrugged. "She knew we shared quarters. She wasn't here for a social visit but to ascend to her spiritual potential. Our private lives were irrelevant."

"What's your real name?"

"Celeste."

"Last name?"

"Ashton."

"Maiden name?"

She stood. "The police have all that information. I have a funeral to plan."

She walked toward the gazebo entrance.

"Just one more question," I said.

She turned, waited.

"Where did you live before coming to Pelican Bay?"

"A better question," she responded in the same flat voice that had failed to come alive during our entire exchange, "is where will I go now?"

She declined, however, to provide an answer for either query. Again in sleepwalking mode, she left the gazebo and crossed the lawn toward the building hidden by trees behind the dining hall.

I left the gazebo and met Bill at the fountain in front of the main building. "Find anything?"

He shook his head. "Just a daylight view of the path beaten through the grove from the street and the profusion of deadly nightshade growing throughout the property. How about you?"

"Celeste claims Alicia had an unrequited love for Ashton, and, since she couldn't have him, she killed him. And would have killed Celeste, too, if she'd been on time for lunch."

"Looks bad for the home team," Bill admitted.

"Apparently Alicia had motive, means and opportunity. And no alibi."

"Celeste has motive, means, and opportunity, too," Bill noted, "but for some reason Keating's letting her off the hook."

"Maybe Celeste passed a polygraph," I said. "She's very convincing when she claims that Alicia's guilty."

Bill sighed. "Unless we can drum up other suspects, like the Hispanic visitor Swinburn ran into, the prosecutor's going to hang Alicia out to dry."

"Garth's stranger may prove as elusive as *The Fugitive*'s one-armed man. Let's hope Hector Morales, the lawn man, can lead us to him."

CHAPTER 12

We left Grove Spirit House, picked up sandwiches at Scallops downtown and stopped at my condo to eat. Roger met us at the door and threw himself at me as if I'd been gone for a month. Roger was a very social pooch who hated when I worked weekends. During the week, if I was out on a call, he stayed with Darcy at the office. On weekends, however, he had to remain alone in the condo. Bill assured me that Roger probably slept the entire time I was away, but his exuberance at my return always made me feel guilty that I'd left him behind.

After finishing lunch, we took Roger for a walk along the waterfront. The onshore breeze and the usual early afternoon drop in humidity made the stroll tolerable. If you could call it a stroll. We had to stop every few feet for Roger to sniff where other dogs had passed and to make his own mark on the territory. No wonder he drank so much. He utilized every drop in his determination to leave calling cards for other canines that used his route.

"Remember," Bill reminded me as we waited for Roger to water a sago palm, "we're invited to the Adlers' for a cookout tonight."

Roger, who I swore understood every word we said, turned around and gazed at us with big sad eyes.

"Don't worry," I assured him. "You're invited, too."

Apparently satisfied, Roger resumed his walk.

"We can ask Adler tonight," I said to Bill, "whether he wants to work security for the wedding reception at Sophia's."

"Damn," Bill said. "With Ashton's murder, I forgot all about the Burns-Baker feud. I'd hoped to talk to the families and get a take on their attitudes before we accept—or decline—the job."

"Why don't you interview Hector Morales this afternoon," I suggested, "and I'll visit the war zone."

"War zone?"

"Pineland Circle, where the Burnses and Bakers live."

"You'll need a cover."

I nodded. "It won't be good for Antonio's business if the feuding families suspect that he doubts they're capable of behaving themselves." I thought for a moment. "I could tell them I'm the events coordinator for Sophia's, visiting to finalize details. I'll go by the restaurant and ask Antonio for a copy of their contract on my way over there."

With Roger's bladder finally depleted, we returned to my place. I unleashed the dog, and Bill went to the phone. Earlier, in the dining hall of Grove Spirit House, he'd found Hector Morales's number scribbled on a note tacked to a bulletin board hanging above the phone. Now he called the number to ask directions. A young boy, who identified himself as Hector's son, said his father was working. When pressed, the kid gave Bill an address.

"Hector's mowing the lawn of one of his clients on Pelican Pointe," Bill said. "I'll see if I can catch him there. And I'll pick you up at six to go to the Adlers'."

Bill left, and Roger moped, dogging my steps as if he was aware that I'd be leaving soon, too. His spirits perked up when he followed me into the kitchen and watched me stuff a hard rubber bone with peanut butter, creating a real doggie dilemma. He didn't want to be abandoned but knew he wouldn't receive his treat unless I departed.

* * *

When I arrived at Pineland Circle, the cul-de-sac where the Burnses and Bakers resided uneasily side by side, I noted instantly one facet of their years-long dispute. The Baker property was well-maintained. The house sparkled with a fresh coat of paint, and the lush lawn and attractive shrubbery had been neatly cut.

The Burnses' residence was a study in contrasts. The carcass of a 1956 Chevy stood on concrete blocks in the side yard, surrounded by weeds. Garbage cans and gardening supplies had been piled haphazardly in front of the double garage doors. The home's walls needed paint; the tile roof was black with mildew; and what should have been a lawn sported large patches of barren sand, punctuated by clumps of sandspurs and weeds.

I'd done some checking on the Burnses. Linda's father owned a plumbing company with a fleet of a dozen trucks. He apparently made good money, so their property's neglected state was a reflection of bad habits rather than lack of income.

Mrs. Burns, a tall, thin woman with skin prematurely aged by sun and cigarettes, one of which dangled from her narrow lips, answered the door. She had her dyed-blond hair pulled back in a scrunchie that accentuated her graying brown roots and wore faded shorts and a skimpy halter top that provided no uplift for her sagging breasts.

"What?" she demanded in a voice hoarse from too many smokes.

I faked a smile and tried to look perky. "I'm Margaret, events coordinator from Sophia's restaurant. Mr. Stavropoulos asked me to stop by to go over the details for Linda's wedding reception." I flashed the copy of the contract to verify my claim. "If now's not a good time, I can come back later."

"Come on in," she said without enthusiasm. "Carl's gone to the hardware store, so now's good. It's best he's not here. He's already griping about how much money this wedding is costing. I don't want to rattle his chain."

She stood aside, and I entered the disaster zone that passed for a living area. Old newspapers, empty beer cans, articles of clothing, stacks of old mail, several large cats and an abundance of cat hair covered every surface and dotted the rug.

Poor woman. A hubby, six kids, and no one to rake the living room.

But the clutter paled into insignificance compared to the overwhelming stench of cat pee. No wonder the woman smoked. She needed something to fend off the smell.

Mrs. Burns swept aside cats and newspapers to clear a spot on the sofa. "Take a load off."

I sat gingerly and breathed through my mouth, as I'd learned to do at crime scenes and autopsies where the victim had been dead for a while. I hoped I could learn what I needed in a hurry, before the urine odors saturated my clothes and hair.

"Are there any additional arrangements you want Sophia's to make for the reception?" I asked.

She took a long drag on her cigarette, then exhaled a lungful of smoke. "Like I said, it's costing too damn much already. Don't try to heap more expenses on us."

"You misunderstand," I explained hastily. "I'm only here to assure that everything goes smoothly, in the way that you intended."

"Holy crap," she said with scowl, "if this wedding was the way I intended, my Linda wouldn't be marrying that Baker brat in the first place."

"I'm sorry." I drenched my voice with sympathy. "I didn't realize there was a problem."

"Damn right there's a problem." Her eyes flashed with malice. "My Linda's hot. She could have any man on the planet, but she chose Kevin Baker. God only knows why."

I threw her an understanding look. "This Kevin isn't...acceptable?"

"He's an attorney."

"You don't like attorneys?"

Mrs. Burns shrugged. "He makes good money, and he's not bad to look at, but Linda could have done better. Could have married wealth and prestige. For a girl with Linda's looks, that's what she deserves."

"So your family isn't happy with the pending marriage?"

Mrs. Burns arched an eyebrow that had been plucked and tortured into a thin line. "You afraid we'll make trouble?"

"No, but bad feelings can cause tension."

"Don't worry, lady. My family knows how to behave themselves. We've tried talking Linda out of this, but if marrying Kevin is what she wants, we'll grit our teeth, paint on smiles, and go along with it. And pay the price, which is too damned much in my book." Her eyebrows lowered and her eyes narrowed. "Can't promise the same for Kevin's folks, though. They've always been troublemakers."

I opened my eyes wide. "Surely you don't think the groom's family would create a scene, not at their own son's wedding?"

Mrs. Burns stubbed out her cigarette and searched through the clutter on the table beside her until she found a half-full pack and lit another. "No, they probably won't cause trouble. Not in public, anyway. Not in front of their fancy friends. They're too status-conscious and holier-than-thou. They'd rather stab us in the back when nobody's looking."

"So even though there are...strained relations between your families, you don't anticipate any problems?"

She sucked on the cigarette until I feared she'd inhale it, too, and blew smoke through her nostrils. "This is my daughter's big day. Kevin's not our choice. Hell, we can't stand him or his family, but we'll do everything to see that Linda's wedding goes off without a hitch."

Without a hitch struck me as an obvious Freudian slip, but I kept a straight face.

"And you don't wish to make any changes to the

reception plans?" I played my coordinator role to the hilt. "Now is your chance, while there's still time."

She shook her head, then glanced at her watch. "My husband will be back soon. I don't want to get him started again on how much money this wedding is costing us."

I forced a smile. "I understand. Thank you for your time."

She showed me to the door, and I hurried outside. After several deep breaths of air that was hot and muggy but untainted by cat urine, I strolled up the front walk of the Baker house next door and rang the bell. While I waited for an answer, I brushed cat hair from my clothes.

A short, plump woman opened the door. "Yes?"

"Mrs. Baker?"

She nodded, a movement that didn't disturb the neat, slightly bouffant arrangement of her brown hair, and gave a warm but tentative smile. She wore a light blue denim patio dress, its sleeveless yoke embroidered with pale pink flamingos, and matching blue sandals that exposed pearly pink toenails. A touch of blush that matched her flawless lipstick highlighted her apple cheeks, and she emanated a whiff of Chanel No. 5.

"I'm Margaret, events coordinator at Sophia's. I'm here to check on details for your son's wedding reception."

Her smile faded to a frown. "There must be some mistake."

"Your son Kevin is marrying Linda Burns, isn't he?"

"Yes, but her family is paying for the reception." Her mouth formed a moue of distaste before she continued. "Any details would be their responsibility."

"Of course." I began my verbal tap dance. "But as a courtesy, Sophia's likes to run the arrangements by the groom's family, to make certain there are no surprises." Again I brandished the contract with Sophia's letterhead to authenticate my ruse.

"How thoughtful of the restaurant," Mrs. Baker said with a genuine smile. "Come in."

I stepped into a living room that looked like the *after* photo in a makeover of the Burnses' disaster area next door. Hardwood floors and oak furniture gleamed; sofas and chairs, cushions plumped and welcoming stood free of clutter. An arrangement of fresh flowers graced the coffee table. And the aroma of baking filled the air.

"Have a seat," Mrs. Baker said. "I'll be right with you as soon as I take the cookies out of the oven."

The woman, whose role models were obviously June Cleaver and Donna Reed, made me feel as if I'd stepped into a time machine and been transported to the 1950s. But a smoothly run household and flawless grooming didn't mean Mrs. Baker couldn't cause trouble. My mother and Caroline were living proof.

While Mrs. Baker was in her kitchen, I studied a row of family photographs, arranged in silver frames along the mantel.

"Those are my children," she said when she returned. She picked up the frame on the far left and handed it to me. "That's Kevin, my oldest."

"He's very handsome." I wasn't just making conversation. The kid could have been a movie star. Not the too-pretty male-model type, but a man's man, handsome with a hint of ruthlessness in the strong angle of his jaw.

I handed her the photo and she replaced it at the proper angle beside the others. When she turned back toward me, her brown eyes swam with unshed tears. "I can't believe my baby is getting married."

Her baby had to be going on thirty. "You're not losing a son. You're gaining a daughter."

Her glossy lips set in a hard, thin line. "I wouldn't call Linda Burns a daughter."

I made a sympathetic noise.

As I'd hoped, Mrs. Burns kept talking. "She's not a nice girl." As if suddenly realizing what she'd said, she clamped a hand over her mouth, then dropped it to her side and shrugged. "But she's Kevin's choice. That's all that matters," she added with strained enthusiasm.

I handed her the copy of the reception-dinner contract. "Would you look over this, please?"

She skimmed through the menu and other details, pausing here and there with a tsk-tsking noise. With a sigh, she returned the papers. "Not the selections I would have made, but then I'm not paying the bill."

"May I be blunt?" I asked.

She looked startled, but nodded. "Please."

"We've heard at Sophia's that there is…tension between your family and the Burnses. Is there any reason to expect problems at the reception?"

Mrs. Baker shook her head and smiled. "Our children squabbled when they were younger, but they're all adults now. And mine, at least, know how to behave, especially in public." She preened with maternal pride. "We can tolerate the Burnses long enough to see Kevin married. Especially since he's so much in love. None of us want to spoil his happiness."

I pushed to my feet. "I've taken too much of your time."

"My pleasure," she said. "Won't you stay and have some cookies and iced tea?"

The freshly baked cookies smelled wonderful. And fattening. "Thanks, but I should get back to work."

I returned to my car and drove away. Hard feelings obviously ran deep between the two families, but both mothers had expressed a desire to suppress them to insure their children's happiness. I could only hope, for Antonio's sake, that their good intentions didn't pave the road to the reception from hell.

CHAPTER 13

Bill showed up at my condo an hour early to take me to the Adlers'.

I greeted him with a kiss. "The cookout's not until six, right?"

"Yes, but I missed you."

"That's always good to hear." I snuggled into his embrace.

Without a doubt, Bill was good for me. In my years as a cop, I'd allowed work to preempt my life, consuming my waking hours, isolating me from family and friends. I'd always had too many open cases and not enough time. In the process, I'd neglected to relax, have fun and luxuriate in doing nothing. Bill had warned me that if our upcoming marriage was to succeed, I'd have to learn new habits. Set in my workaholic ways, I was trying to reform. So instead of asking about his interview with Hector Morales, I offered Bill a beer.

"You actually have something consumable in your refrigerator?" he responded in surprise.

"At least a beer." I hoped. I couldn't remember the last time I'd looked.

"Sure, I'll have one."

I grabbed a Michelob and a Diet Coke from the otherwise empty fridge and followed him into the living room. We sat on the rattan sofa opposite the sliding glass doors that overlooked St. Joseph Sound where the channel was filled with boats returning to dock after a Saturday on the Gulf of Mexico.

Bill sipped his beer and glanced around the room. "Have you thought about how much of this furniture you want to keep?"

Bill had always teased me about my taste in decorating, calling it typical Florida-hotel style, but I loved the cool tropical blues and greens and the airy wicker and rattan. Mostly, I had to admit, I liked the status quo, and the thought of chucking belongings that had been with me for more than a dozen years made me slightly queasy.

"No," I said. "What's the hurry? We're not moving into the new house until after the wedding."

"No hurry, but you might want to start thinking

about it. Maybe next week we can drive over to Plant City and pick out furniture from my folks' house that we'll want to keep. They had quite a few mission-style Stickley pieces that will look great in our new place. But only if you want them."

What I wanted was the way things were. Not because I didn't love Bill, but because, under the current circumstances, he loved me and we got along just fine. I didn't want to do anything that would damage that balance. Luckily, Bill had agreed on a long engagement to give me time to get used to the idea of marriage and a shift in lifelong habits.

He was watching, waiting for an answer, his head cocked slightly to one side, with the crooked smile that quirked the corners of his mouth, and a sparkle in those baby blues that made my heart melt. God, I didn't want to screw things up, but my track record with relationships, from my mother and sister to my former chief, was not reassuring.

"We'll check out the Stickley," I said, diving blindly into the unfamiliar, but adding quickly, "only if we can take time from the case."

I'd been sabotaged by my insecurities. What I'd wanted to say was that I'd go anywhere with him, do anything he wished, any time, but I'd fallen back into the safety of the rut of work.

A frown flickered briefly across that face I loved so much before he smiled again and nodded. "Alicia Langston is counting on us."

I'd opened the door, stumbled back into old habits, and didn't have the sense or courage to back off. "So, what did you find out from Morales this afternoon?"

"Not much that will be helpful unless we can get our hands on the roster of Grove Spirit House's clients. In the months he's worked there, Hector told me that hundreds of people, mostly women, have taken the Ashtons' seminars, some attending only for an afternoon, others staying weeks or more."

"Did he recall any of them causing problems?"

Bill shook his head.

"Arguments between Willard and Celeste?"

"Nada. He did mention that in the past few months Celeste has left the compound for a few nights every week to visit her mother."

"Trouble in paradise?" I asked.

Bill shrugged. "Hector didn't know. He was only there a few hours a week, and, according to him, their usual behavior was loco, so how could he tell if they were having problems?"

Hector made a good point. "Had he seen the bald Hispanic guy with the scar who Garth ran into?"

"No, and he knew of no one who fits that description who lives in the area."

"Maybe the guy wasn't Hispanic," I said. "Maybe he spoke Spanish to conceal his identity."

"If there really was an intruder."

"You think Garth lied?"

Bill wiped condensation from his beer bottle against the leg of his cargo shorts. "Swinburn seems like a good kid, but we've known plenty of good people pushed off the deep end by extraordinary circumstances. No man likes the humiliation of being dumped. We have to consider the possibility that Garth could be covering something."

I nodded. Until we had incontrovertible proof of guilt, everyone was a suspect, from Garth to Celeste to Morales, and even Alicia, our client. But our investigation had hit a wall. Unless Adler had run across something in his crime databases, so far we had nothing concrete to offer Terry Pender for Alicia's defense.

"What's the verdict on the Hatfields and McCoys?" Bill asked.

I described my visits with Mrs. Burns and Mrs. Baker. "I think we can handle them, if Adler and Mackley help, and if we have a contingency plan in case of trouble."

"No signs of all-out war?"

"The families' dislike of one another was obvious in my conversations with the matriarchs. But most of their kids are adults now. We can only hope that with maturity, they've learned some self-control."

"Hell, Margaret, if chronological maturity equaled self-control, cops would be out of a job."

Unable to argue with that wisdom, I went to feed Roger, who was already in the kitchen, turning circles by his food dish.

Bill parked his SUV in front of Adler's house. I climbed out and released Roger from the backseat. The pooch, who had been here before, stopped only once to lift his leg on a clump of the liriope that lined the sidewalk before making a beeline to the front porch.

The Adler house, pale gray clapboards with gleaming black shutters, was small but big on charm and warmth. The curving brick walk led to a welcoming farmhouse porch filled with rocking chairs, a swing and pots of bright red geraniums. More than a residence, it had *home* written all over it. Its appeal, along with our fondness for the Adlers, had prompted our earlier search in this same neighborhood for our own home, which we had found just a couple of blocks away.

Jessica, fast approaching her second birthday, waited on the porch with her mother. Roger bounded up the steps in his funny drunken-sailor gait, ran straight for the toddler and swiped her face with his tongue.

With giggles of delight, Jessica sat with a thud and grabbed Roger by the ears. "Woger tickle!"

Jessica and Roger had played before, but afraid he might nip her in his excitement, I picked him up and tucked him under my arm. Sharon lifted Jessica.

"Good to see you guys," she said. "Glad you could come. Dave's out back at the grill."

Sharon, petite and pretty with green eyes and dark brown hair, waved us inside to the family room. I noted that her pregnancy had barely begun to show beneath the loose T-shirt she wore over her shorts.

"We could sit on the deck," she offered, "but it's steaming hot out there, even in the shade."

"In here is fine," Bill said.

I settled on the sofa; Jessica scrambled up beside me, and Roger, lured by the scent of cooking, pressed his smushed-in nose against a glass pane in the rear door and drooled.

Through the wall-to-wall French doors across the back of the family room, I could see Adler at the gas grill, brushing barbecue sauce on chicken. Dressed in shorts, a faded Pelican Bay Police Department T-shirt, and barefooted, he had the good looks of a young soap star. That thick, shaggy hair, those innocent eyes and his fresh-faced charm had lulled people he'd investigated into assuming there was no substance behind his handsome facade, but Adler was one of the best detectives I knew, and the Clearwater PD was lucky to have him. He'd been a great partner, and I missed him.

Hell, I missed the whole department, even Chief Shelton, who'd made my life miserable every day of the fifteen-plus years I'd served with Pelican Bay. Working as a private investigator with Bill had its own rewards, but it wasn't, and Bill would be the first to agree with me, the same as being a cop.

Sharon served iced tea in tall glasses. Outside,

Adler adjusted the temperature control on the grill, then joined us.

"Hey," he greeted us. "Food'll be ready in about fifteen minutes."

"I'll toss the salad." Sharon returned to the kitchen area, separated from the family room by a breakfast bar.

Jessica crawled from me to Bill, who welcomed her with open arms. She patted Bill's face with her pudgy hands. "Play horsey," she demanded.

He sat her astride his shin and bounced her up and down until she crowed with delight.

The look of longing on Bill's face was almost painful to witness because I knew what he was thinking. Bill had been married when I'd first met him, and his only child, a daughter, had been six years old. Shortly after I'd saved his life during a domestic call, his wife Trish had filed for divorce, no longer able to endure the fears of every police officer's spouse, that someday her husband would end his shift in a body bag. She'd been granted primary custody of their daughter Melanie, and they had moved to Seattle. Bill had tried to keep in touch with his daughter, but thousands of miles and her eventual shift of loyalties to her new stepdad had driven a wedge between them.

Melanie had eventually broken all contact with her father, and although now married with a family of her own, she'd never encouraged Bill to visit his granddaughters.

It was a crying shame. Bill would have made the world's best granddad. I could tell, just watching him with Jessica.

"Before I forget," Adler said, "I have something for you."

He went to a desk beside the fireplace and removed a folder from the top drawer. "Got some hits on your Willard Ashton."

"You're a better man than me." Bill shifted his attention momentarily from Jessica. "I struck out."

"Not your fault." Adler handed me the folder. "Apparently the sheriff's office did, too, at first. So Doc Cline had to fingerprint the body to make the identification. Once the SO matched the prints in AFIS, aliases started popping up like warts on a frog."

I took the folder, opened it and studied the printouts. A color photo of Willard Ashton stared back at me from the first page, not the bald Mr. Clean I'd met, but a younger man with wavy black hair. The name under the mug shot was Richard Cooper with an address in Fort White, Florida. A scan of the three-year-old incident report indicated he'd been charged with assault after a dustup with one of his former clients at River Spirit House, located on the Sante Fe River outside of Fort White.

Bill placed Jessica in her playpen, and I handed him that report and went on to the next. It contained a photo of an even younger Ashton, this one named James Bessemer, with blond hair. The charge, filed in Walhalla, South Carolina, in relation to Bessemer's retreat at Mountain Spirit House, included a claim by a local resident that she'd been sexually molested. Authorities, unable to resolve the he-said/she-said, dilemma, had released Bessemer.

The last report showed a mug shot of a young man in his late teens, arrested for a series of petty crimes in Nashville, Tennessee. His name was Ryan Wayne and he'd been sentenced to five years in state prison for car theft. An attached sheet indicated he hadn't been a model prisoner and had been disciplined for several altercations with his fellow inmates. Apparently the young Ashton hadn't yet learned the peace and tranquillity of oneness with the Universal Spirit.

So Willard Ashton's real name was Ryan Wayne, but he'd also used Richard Cooper and James Bessemer as aliases when he'd moved his scam to new locations.

Bill finished reading the last sheet. "Looks like there's no shortage of people with motive to kill Ashton. He left a trail of discontent that goes back almost two decades."

I nodded. "We have our work cut out for us."

Adler sprang to his feet from his recliner by the fireplace. "The chicken should be ready."

He went out to the grill, and Sharon set serving bowls on the pine table in the eat-in kitchen. "Come and get it, guys."

Later, finished with my meal, I watched Adler, who'd consumed half a large chicken, a mountain of potato salad and several crusty rolls, dig into a man-sized slice of lemon meringue pie. In almost every memory I had of him as my partner, he'd been eating something. How he kept his fighting trim with that appetite, I couldn't figure. Grocery bills had probably bankrupted his family when Adler had gone through his growth spurts as a teen.

I added two spoons of sugar to my coffee. "Thanks for Ashton's rap sheets," I said to Adler. "We'd hit a dead end in our investigation, and the sheriff's office won't give up anything yet."

"Who's their detective on the case?" Adler asked.

"Guy named Garrett Keating," Bill said. "You know him?"

Adler shook his head. "Must be new to the SO. They've filled a lot of vacancies recently, created by retirements. If he's new, my guess is he'll be hard-nosed and play everything strictly by the book until he's more familiar with the job." He passed his plate to Sharon, who loaded it with another slice of pie.

"Anyone else want more?" she asked.

"No thanks," Bill said, "but it was delicious, as always."

I shook my head.

"Anything more I can do to help?" Adler asked before digging into his second dessert.

Now seemed as good a time as any to bring up the Burns-Baker bash. I looked to Bill, and he nodded.

"Want to earn some overtime?" I said.

I caught Sharon's frown out of the corner of my eye and knew what she was thinking. Adler's regular job in homicide kept him working long hours, so he had little time to spend with his family.

"This is only one evening," I explained quickly, "and the pay's good."

I quoted the rate, and Adler whistled. "That *is* good, and we could use some extra funds, what with the new baby and all."

"Is it dangerous?" Sharon asked.

"Security for a wedding reception," Bill explained.

Sharon looked puzzled. "Who's getting married, the child of a Mafia boss?"

I shook my head. "Kevin Baker and Linda Burns."

Adler groaned. "Of Pineland Circle?"

"You remember them, of course."

"Any officer who's patrolled Pelican Bay remembers them," Adler said. "I can't believe those families will be joined by marriage. No wonder you need security for the reception."

"It's at Sophia's the last Saturday of the month," I said. "And Antonio wants to make sure there's no trouble."

Adler grinned. "I understand now why you're paying so much. Hazardous duty."

"How hazardous?" Sharon insisted.

"Probably more boring than hazardous," I said. "The kids in both families are grown now. And their mothers insist their broods will be on their best behavior for the happy couple's sake."

Adler cast a glance at Sharon before looking back at me. "I'll check my schedule and let you know Monday."

"Fine," Bill said. "Abe Mackley's retired from the Tampa PD. We thought we'd ask him to join us, too."

I saw the look that passed between Sharon and Adler and knew he'd ask her opinion before accepting or declining our offer. Adler was not only a good cop, but a good husband. Divorce rates for police officers were astronomical, but the Adlers worked hard for a good chance of defying the odds.

I glanced at Bill, laughing at Sharon's tale of Jessica's latest exploits, and wondered what chance of success our coming marriage would have. Neither of us was a cop any longer, but we'd been forever influenced by the job, right down to our bones.

As if reading my thoughts, Bill turned and bestowed on me a reassuring expression that temporarily sent my misgivings up in flames.

In that brief moment, Bill's prior suggestion of eloping immediately seemed like a good idea.

CHAPTER 14

By dawn the next morning, my usual doubts and misgivings over commitment had replaced my euphoria
and optimism of the night before. In the cozy comfort
of the Adler home, watching Adler and Sharon inter-
act, believing in happily-ever-after had been easy.

But awaking in my solitary bed in my condo, listening to the gulls fighting over food in the tidal flats outside my window, I couldn't picture waking up every
morning beside Bill. Not that I didn't want to. I
couldn't imagine anything better. But what if I couldn't
break myself of lifelong habits?

Even now my brain churned with the what-ifs and
possibilities of the Ashton case, and I couldn't turn it off.

Easier, my conscience pricked me, to deal with murder suspects than your own problems. Easier to trace
leads than to loosen up and find ways to have fun.

"Shut up," I told myself.

I nudged aside Roger, who slept curled against my legs, tossed back the covers and headed for the shower.

Bill was catching a flight to Nashville this morning to check out the checkered past of Ryan Wayne, aka Willard Ashton. After dropping Bill at the airport, I'd drive to Fort White to interview the guy who'd engaged in a slugfest with Ashton back when he was called Richard Cooper and operating a retreat on the Santa Fe River.

Before I made it to the shower, the phone by my bed rang.

Expecting Bill, I answered in my sexiest tone.

"Margaret," Mother's scandalized voice rang in my ear. "Have you been drinking?"

I intentionally misunderstood. "Haven't had my coffee yet."

"Well, I'm glad I found you at home."

I glanced at the bedside clock. Where else would I be at 6:15 on a Sunday morning?

"I called," she continued, "to invite you and your young man to have lunch at the club."

"Sorry, Mo—" I caught myself before calling her *Mom*, an appellation she considered common and had forbidden me to use "——ther, but my young man is catching a plane in a couple hours for Tennessee."

Her sigh of disapproval reverberated in my ear. "But you'll come, of course? You never spend time with me."

Either she'd already forgotten our recent lunch, or somehow it hadn't counted in the scheme of daughterly obligations. "I'm heading for North Florida as soon as I drop Bill at the airport. We're working a case."

"Really, Margaret, what's the point of being in business for yourself if you don't take weekends off?"

"It's these inconsiderate criminals. They have no sense of decorum."

"Be serious," she said with a snap of impatience. "I really must speak with you about the wedding."

"And I need to talk with you, Mother."

I was tempted to delay my trip, join her at the club, and lay down the law about canceling her fancy plans. But only because she'd be less likely to skin me alive in front of witnesses. However, the trail for Willard Ashton's killer was getting colder by the minute, and I couldn't afford the delay.

"Just promise me one thing," I asked her.

"What?"

"That you won't sign anything with Madame Lapierre or make any other commitments until we've talked."

"Of course not. After all, dear, it is *your* wedding."

I laughed aloud at the righteous indignation in her tone.

"If you don't take these details seriously—" words of steel from a velvet larynx "—you'll be too late to make the proper arrangements."

"That's what I need to talk to you about. I'll call when I get back in town."

"Be sure you do."

She hung up without a goodbye, much less *drive carefully, take care,* or *I love you.*

I wasn't expecting such sentiments. Intellectually, I understood that she probably wasn't capable of expressing them, but how much I wanted to hear them was pathetic.

I showered and dressed quickly, then took Roger and his assortment of toys, dishes, food and doggy lounger to Darcy's. He loved riding in the car and would have enjoyed the upcoming trip, but, so far, PBI had no need for an untrained K-9. If Roger caught a criminal, he'd either lick him senseless or hump his leg. At least, due to Darcy's hospitality, the poor pooch was spared the slammer at the vet's when I had to be away overnight.

When I left Darcy's house, she was plying him with his favorite bone-marrow treats. The fickle pup didn't even whine when I drove away, which proved what I'd always suspected: the way to Roger's devotion was through his stomach.

After picking up Bill and dropping him at Departures at Tampa International Airport, I retraced my route toward the causeway and hung a right on the Suncoast Parkway, a toll road that would take me north of the Bay area, avoiding the worst of the traffic. The route passed through cypress swamps and cattle pastures, where the occasional clearing or plywood walls shrouded in Tyvek popped up like the first pustules in the erupting plague of development. Recent news articles had reported that more than 150,000 acres statewide, an area the size of Pinellas County, had fallen prey to new building in the past year. And people continued to flock in droves to live in Florida, blissfully ignoring the fact that with each new arrival, more of what attracted them here in the first place withered and died beneath the crush of bulldozers, concrete and asphalt.

I shook off my annoyance and resolved to enjoy the scenery while I could. I was instantly rewarded by the sight of a herd of Brahman cattle, which used to roam Pinellas pastures by the thousands. Elegant white cattle egrets sat upon their backs, pecking for insects, and rare whooping cranes scouted for food in a roadside drainage ditch.

The peace and tranquillity of the rural setting had only begun to work its magic when the Parkway dumped me onto U.S. 19 north of Brooksville, and I was once again in a concrete jungle and tangles of traffic. I white-knuckled it to north of Crystal River, where civilization gave way to desolate pine forests all the way to Chiefland. In that sleepy little town, I went through the drive-through at McDonald's for a Diet Coke and burger.

Eating as I drove, I took a secondary road that ran northeast toward Fort White, and soon I was back in cattle country, pockmarked by For Sale signs and billboards advertising homesites available in soon-to-be massive subdivisions.

Since before the Civil War, Florida had been cattle country. The term *cracker* originated with the snap of the early drovers' whips, and even today, Florida was the fourth-largest cattle producer in the nation. But with the subdividing of range lands, soon more beef products, just like oranges, would be imported from South America than grown in the Sunshine State.

Following the map Bill had printed out from his computer, south of Fort White I turned left at the entrance to River Tree Estates and followed a paved road shaded by arching oaks for a few hundred yards before it morphed into a crushed-shell drive. A few hundred yards farther, I found the street I was looking for and turned right onto another shell surface. The lots along the drive were huge, and the houses tucked away among oaks, pines, palmettos and wax myrtles, but I could tell by the occasional glimpse of stilted structures on my left that these homes fronted the Sante Fe River.

I navigated around potholes and an errant armadillo and searched for the address of Gerald Shively, the guy who had duked it out with Ryan Wayne when he'd been posing as Richard Cooper, before he'd become Willard Ashton, at River Spirit House a few miles north of my current location. Ahead, the street ended in a clump of underbrush, and on the left, *Shively* had been written in twisted rebar atop a huge rusty mailbox of dinged and dented tin.

Shively's unpaved driveway meandered around clumps of trees and palmettos before ending abruptly in front of a large shed, its rust-streaked metal roof supported by what looked like the trunks of cabbage palms. I could see through the building, open on all sides, to the river beyond and the main house to the right. An old pickup truck, its bed loaded with scrap metal, was parked among the stilts that protected the house from rising waters. A blue tarp partially covered the junk and hid the license plate.

In the shed, a man dressed only in denim shorts, sandals and a welder's helmet was torching the carcass of an old washing machine in a dazzling display of flying sparks. When I parked in front of the open building and stepped from my car, he turned off his equipment and flipped up his protective mask.

"You lost, lady?"

I waved a hand in front of my face, which did nothing to disperse the cloud of no-see-ums that had formed around my head. "I'm looking for Gerald Shively."

"You found him."

I tried to judge Shively's age, but with his tall, wiry build, skin tanned and desiccated by the sun, and dirty-blond hair pulled back in a ponytail, he could have been anywhere from thirty to fifty. One thing was certain: he wasn't the short, bald, scar-faced Hispanic Garth claimed to have seen. But I hadn't expected to find Swinburn's hostile stranger. That would have been too easy.

"You here to commission work?" Shively asked.

I glanced around the shed at the bizarre sculptures, combinations of old appliances, mufflers, barbed wire and tire rims, welded into various unrecognizable shapes and sizes. I didn't know art, but I knew what I liked, and this wasn't it.

I pulled my ID from my purse and showed it to him. "I'm investigating Willard Ashton."

"Then you are lost, 'cause I never heard of him." With a snap of his head, Shively lowered his face shield to end our conversation.

"Also known as Richard Cooper."

With an exaggerated sigh, Shively removed his helmet and tucked it under his arm. "Cooper, the scam artist. What do you want to know?"

"Why did he assault you?"

"It's in the police report."

"I'd rather hear it from you."

"Lady, I've got work to do."

"Give me the condensed version then."

I was picking up strange vibes from Shively, which could have been his intense dislike of Cooper/Ashton or something more sinister. I hoped if I kept him talking, I'd figure him out.

"Short version—I asked for my money back from his so-called retreat. He refused. I threatened to sue. He hit me."

"You attended one of River Spirit House's retreats?" Although nominally an artist, Shively didn't seem the type to meld meekly with the Universe. He had a cold, hard edge that screamed, "Back off," a definite impediment to oneness.

His face contorted with disgust. "Believe me, participating in that farce wasn't my idea. I told her the retreat was a bunch of crap."

"Her?"

"My wife. We'd been having problems. Then this weirdo complex opens on the river north of here and offers seminars on renewing your marriage. Jayne insisted we give it a try or she was leaving."

"Rock and a hard place," I commiserated.

"Exactly."

He was warming to his subject now, so I let him rant.

"Turned out, Cooper's idea of saving my marriage was boinking my wife. When I caught them, he had the nerve to claim it would loosen her inhibitions, help her better relate to the marriage bed."

I made a sound of outrage mixed with sympathy.

"I kicked the cheating slut out of our marriage bed. That was bad enough. But the creep had charged me five thousand dollars to screw my wife. That really hurt."

At least he had his priorities straight. "Insult to injury."

"Damned right. That's when I demanded my money back."

"But you didn't get it."

Shively shook his head.

"You lost the suit?"

"I didn't sue. Jayne begged me not to. She didn't want the humiliation of a public trial that would reveal her indiscretions. I promised that if she didn't clean me out in the divorce settlement, I wouldn't sue. But I did charge the bastard with assault."

"If you kept his philandering quiet, why did Ashton...er, Cooper close River Spirit House?"

"Turns out my wife wasn't the only woman Cooper

had diddled. When a range of charges was filed by several others, Cooper, vermin that he was, closed operations here and disappeared into the woodwork."

"And you've never seen him since?"

Shively raised his chin and looked me in the eye with an unwavering glance. "Never. And you never said why you're asking questions about him."

"He's dead."

Shock registered on Shively's weather-beaten face, and he sat abruptly on the old washer he'd been torching. "No shit?"

The man was either world class at faking or he was genuinely surprised.

"What was it?" Shively regained his composure enough to ask. "His heart?"

"In a manner of speaking. It stopped when somebody murdered him."

"Murder? You don't think I—"

"Tell me where you were Wednesday and Thursday of last week."

Wariness replaced the shock on his face. "I was here, working."

"You never left your house?"

"Sure, for groceries and to visit junkyards, looking for materials." He jerked his thumb toward his truck. "Found 'em, too. You can see for yourself."

"Mind if I take a look?"

"I got nothing to hide." His body language was contradicting him.

I walked to the truck bed and flipped up the tarp. The license was a specialty tag, Save the Manatee.

I was adding two and two and coming up with three. The truck and tag fit Garth's description of the vehicle he'd seen at Grove Spirit House, but no way could the kid have confused Shively with a short, bald Hispanic with a scar on his face.

"You ever loan your truck to someone else?"

He shook his head. "It's my only means of transportation. Out here in the boonies, I never know when I might need it."

He could have been telling the truth. Or not. Hell, I was good, but I wasn't infallible.

"A man was spotted at Ashton's," I said, "the night before the murder."

"They think he did it?" Shively asked.

"He's a person of interest. The police would like to talk to him." I was making things up as I went along.

Keating had no desire to investigate further. He was satisfied Alicia was his killer.

"What's their person of interest got to do with me?"

"Depends. You know a Hispanic male, short, bald, scar on his cheek?"

Shively paused a moment, then shook his head. "The area is crawling with Mexicans. They mow lawns, work for contractors. They even sneak through the properties along the river to fish. But I don't pay that much attention to what they look like."

My gut said Shively knew more than he was telling, but I had no leverage to make him talk.

"That's it, then. Thanks for your time." I turned to leave.

"Wait."

I looked back, hoping he'd had a change of heart and was ready to tell all.

"As long as you're here, you want to buy a sculpture?"

I glanced around the shed to pick out the ugliest of his works, a hard choice considering the competition, and contemplated buying the monstrosity for Mother, the art connoisseur, as payback for the grief she was giving me over my wedding.

I pointed to a pile of tire rims, a muffler, a battery,

broken headlights and other detritus bound together by welds, baling wire and old battery cables, hands down the tackiest of his creations. It was too big to transport in my Volvo, but maybe, with his pickup, he delivered.

"Ah," he said, "good choice. I call it *Eternity*."

Death on the Highway was a better description, but what did I know?

"How much?" I asked.

"Eight thousand."

I shook my head. "Guess I'm not ready for *Eternity* yet."

Before he could pitch me a cheaper piece, I hurried to my car.

CHAPTER 15

Ten minutes after leaving Shively, I stopped at a convenience store in Fort White to use the pay phone to call Alicia's attorney. Terry Pender answered her cell on the first ring.

"Do you have access to a sketch artist?" I asked.

"Yeah, a guy retired from NYPD who's done some work for me in the past. What do you need?"

"A sketch of the Hispanic male Swinburn saw at Grove Spirit House the night before Ashton died. You think your man could draw that up for me today?"

"I'll get Garth and the artist together and have them work on it. Any luck so far?"

"Nothing specific. Just bad vibes. I'm driving to South Carolina to meet Bill, swap notes and interview another one of Ashton's former clients."

"How can I reach you?"

"Bill has a cell phone." I gave her the number.

"I'll fax you the sketch as soon as I have it."

"How's Alicia holding up?" I asked.

"Not good. The shock is wearing off and she's going to pieces."

"I need to talk to her as soon as I get back."

"I'll arrange it," Terry said. "Good luck."

It was almost 10:00 p.m. when I met Bill at a motel at the intersection of I-85 and U.S. 441, north of Commerce, Georgia. He had already turned in the rental car he'd driven from Nashville and booked a room with a refrigerator and microwave. He'd also picked up dinner before the restaurants had closed.

While I related my interview with Shively, he heated entrées in the microwave and removed salads from the fridge.

I sat at the table opposite Bill and dug into my salad. I'd had nothing to eat since McDonald's. If I'd been on my own, I'd have been consuming crackers and a Diet Coke from the vending machine, but Bill always made certain I was well-fed, another of the multitude of things I loved about him.

"Shively's truck fits Swinburn's description." I ate

another mouthful. "And Shively had motive, but where does this Hispanic guy come in?"

I pointed to the sketch of the scar-faced male Terry had faxed to the motel office.

"Hired hit man?" Bill suggested.

"It's possible. If Shively's actually selling his junk for the kind of prices he quoted me, he could afford a hired killer."

"But hit men usually kill with a bullet to the head," Bill said. "Poison's generally a woman's weapon."

I nodded. "My money's on Celeste, but we have nothing concrete. Maybe this Hispanic, if we find him, can help us nail down her motive."

"We'll stop in Fort White again on our way home," Bill said. "Show this sketch around and see if anyone can ID him. Meanwhile, I have my own theory on Baldie's identity."

"Something you turned up in Tennessee on Ashton's past as Ryan Wayne?"

Bill nodded. "Wayne was far from a model prisoner. He was always fighting with other inmates. In one brawl he cut open a guy's face with a shiv."

"A Hispanic?"

"Jorges Garcia."

"Bald?"

"Not twenty years ago, according to the warden's records."

I stared at the ragged scar across the cheek of the man in the sketch. "This guy might not be bald, either. A lot of tough guys shave their heads these days."

"But if he's so tough," Bill said, "how come he slipped poison into Ashton's food? Not much machismo in that."

"If Shively hired him—" too damned many *ifs* "—Shively could have wanted maximum damage to Ashton. Kill him, his wife and his clients. And cover his tracks by laying the blame on the kitchen help."

"Makes sense," Bill said with a nod. "Only one problem."

"What's that?"

"Where the hell *is* Garcia?"

I thought for a moment. "We can call Adler. Ask him to run the name through DMV. If Garcia has a Florida driver's license, it will give us an address."

Bill grinned. "The way your brain works, you should be a detective."

"Bite your tongue," I said, "and pass the manicotti."

* * *

The next morning, Bill and I arrived in Walhalla, a charming little town in northwest South Carolina, around 9:30 a.m. I appreciated the cool crispness of the mountain air, a welcome change from Florida's suffocating humidity. We stopped for coffee at a small café and asked directions to the address of Cynthia Woods, the she-said half of the sexual-assault charge against Ashton, known then as James Bessemer.

We left the coffee shop and soon found the address that had been listed in the police report, a handsome three-story brick house on a one-acre landscaped lot with a gated entry and sweeping front drive. But Cynthia Woods no longer lived there. The maid who answered the door must have had similar inquiries because she immediately responded with an address and directions.

We finally located Cynthia in a run-down trailer park on the edge of town. Her place was an aging double-wide with half the skirting missing and a six-year-old Mercedes looking out of place beneath the attached makeshift carport.

A woman with red-rimmed eyes, tangled hair, and dressed in jeans and a faded sweatshirt answered my knock on the door. Because Cynthia had charged Wayne/Cooper/Bessemer/Ashton with rape, Bill had decided to wait in the car. He figured Cynthia would open up more freely to another woman.

"Yeah?" The half-empty beer bottle in her hand explained the slur in her voice, one giant step beyond Southern drawl.

"Cynthia Woods?" I asked.

"That's me."

She must have seen my glance at the beer in her hand. She shrugged. "It's five o'clock somewhere."

I showed her my ID and introduced myself. "My partner's in the car. We're here to ask some questions about James Bessemer."

"What's the creep done now?" She didn't ask me in, but stepped onto the landing of the rickety steps and pulled the door closed behind her.

"Tell me about your experiences at Mountain Spirit House."

"Experiences?" she said with a harsh laugh. "That's too nice a word for it. I was raped."

I nodded. "I read the police report. You said Bessemer drugged you."

"Had to. I wouldn't submit to him like the others.

He claimed I couldn't achieve oneness with the Universal Spirit without the outward physical manifestations. In other words, sex with him."

"What brought you to the retreat in the first place?"

She rotated the bottle, sloshing beer against the sides. "I was bored. You can't tell from looking at me now, but I was the pretty, pampered wife of the owner of a successful car dealership. My children were at college, I could only have my hair and nails done so many times a month, and I was going out of my mind. When Bessemer and his wife opened Mountain Spirit House, their retreat seemed like the answer to a prayer." Tears formed in her bleary eyes. "Turned out to be a curse."

"His wife? Bessemer was married then?"

Cynthia nodded. "Celeste was his business manager. And she took care of the male clients."

"Took care of?"

"The whole damned business was about nothing but sex. *Universal oneness* was a euphemism for one huge orgy. And Bessemer strutted around the place like a randy rooster."

"Celeste was okay with that?" I was having trouble

picturing the woman I'd met with the one Cynthia had described.

Cynthia shook her head. "Didn't matter whether Celeste was okay with it or not. I could tell she was terrified of her husband. And after I filed charges and saw his temper explode, I understood why."

"Did others—"

"Margaret," Bill called from the car. He opened the door and approached with his cell phone. "Call for you. It's Caroline."

My heart jammed in my throat. Caroline had Bill's cell number in case of emergencies, and Bill wouldn't have interrupted my interrogation if the call hadn't been important.

I met him halfway and took the phone. "It's me, Maggie."

"I've just brought Mother to the emergency room," Caroline said. "She's asking for you. You'd better come home."

"Another stroke?" Worry and guilt made me sick to my stomach.

"It's her heart. How soon can you get here?"

I was more than six hundred miles away. "I'll check the airlines. Tell her we're on our way."

* * *

The nearest airports were Greenville, Asheville and Atlanta, all hours away. By the time we could have reached any of them and I made connecting flights to Tampa, Bill figured he could drive me home as quickly. We left Walhalla shortly after noon.

Guilt gnawed at me. "I shouldn't have given her such a hard time about the wedding. She's only been out of the hospital two months."

"You didn't cause your mother's illness," Bill assured me.

I wished I felt as certain. She'd made her unhappiness clear in her last phone call. I'd refused to meet her for lunch. If she died...

"Concentrate on the Ashton case," Bill appealed to the workaholic side of my nature to suppress the neurotic daughter. "Tell me everything we know. What fits, what doesn't. We have to get a handle on this for Alicia's sake."

"How can I think about work, when my mother—"

"May be perfectly fine by the time we get there." Bill wasn't hard-hearted. He was trying to distract me.

I took a deep breath, said a silent prayer for

Mother's recovery, and did as he asked. "Assuming Alicia is innocent, our main suspects are Garth—"

"Motive?"

"Jealousy and/or revenge. Ashton stole the affections of his fiancée. And their honeymoon account. Garth had the means and opportunity, since, by his own admission, he was in the grove the night before Ashton died."

"Probability that he's our man?" Bill kept his eyes on the road, but I could almost hear the wheels turning in his brain. He'd thought through the details of the case, but having someone else's perspective sometimes jogged his mind to take a different tack.

"Hard to tell. Garth seems like a nice kid, but learning about Alicia and Ashton and the missing money might have pushed him over the edge."

We had crossed into Georgia on I-85 and the lush greenness of the open countryside was broken only by the occasional billboard. Although Bill was driving slightly over the speed limit, the car seemed to crawl, making me wonder if we'd ever reach Florida.

"Next suspect?" Bill asked.

"Celeste. She also had means and opportunity. And

Cynthia Woods said Celeste was afraid of Ashton. And she couldn't have been happy with his infidelity."

"Maybe their marriage wasn't a real union but merely part of their scam," Bill said, "especially if their retreats were supposed to be couples' seminars."

"A pretend marriage might rule out jealousy as a motive, but not her fear of Ashton."

"Why not just run away?" he said. "Celeste was the bookkeeper and had access to the money. She could have simply taken what she needed and disappeared."

"We need to know more about her. I'll check with Keating to see if he'll give me her true identity."

We turned south onto U.S. 441 and took the bypass around Athens. Heavy rain from a sudden thunderstorm almost obscured the road ahead, and the wipers of my Volvo flicked at high speed across the windshield.

"So who's your best pick for Ashton's murderer?" Bill asked.

"Jorges Garcia. It's too much of a coincidence this enemy from Ashton's past shows up the night before he dies."

"Motive?"

I thought for a moment. "Maybe the beef he had

with Ryan Wayne in prison has festered all these years. Garcia would be reminded of it every time he saw his scarred cheek in the mirror. With Wayne on the move and changing aliases, it might have taken Garcia this long to catch up with him."

Bill nodded but didn't take his eyes from the road. "Time enough for his hatred to have cooled from hot passion to cold-blooded revenge."

"Hence the poisoning rather than a machismo face-to-face killing."

"What about Shively as a suspect?"

"Garcia could have met Shively when he was tracking Ryan Wayne. Or not. We don't know for sure that Garcia borrowed Shively's truck. He could have used his own vehicle. Old pickups with specialty tags aren't that uncommon."

We'd driven out of the thunderstorm, and Bill switched off the wipers and headlights. Steam rose from the highway where cold rain had met hot asphalt. A recently cleared field on the side of the road revealed red clay, looking like an open wound on the landscape.

"Maybe Shively and Garcia are co-conspirators," Bill suggested. "What if Shively drove Garcia to

Pelican Bay and waited in the truck as lookout while Garcia planted the poison."

"Possible," I agreed. "But my gut tells me we're missing something."

"We have to do more digging. Meantime, why don't you try to get some sleep."

I felt too keyed up to rest, but eventually the hum of the tires on the road, the boring scenery and the soft music on the radio lulled me into slumber.

CHAPTER 16

We arrived in Pelican Bay at 11:00 p.m. and Bill drove straight to the hospital.

I'd called Caroline mid-afternoon but she'd had no news. The doctors were still running tests. After 8:00 p.m., the hospital switchboard had refused to put through calls to Mother's room, so Bill dropped me at the hospital entrance, and I hurried through the empty corridors, not knowing what I'd find, while he parked the car.

Caroline stepped out of Mother's room to meet me in the hall. We walked together to the waiting area, away from sleeping patients.

"She's sleeping." My sister sank into a vinyl-covered chair and looked as if she could use some rest herself. "I tried calling Bill's cell several times, but you must have been in dead zones, because I couldn't reach you."

I sat beside her. "What's her prognosis?"

Caroline rolled her eyes. "Gas."

"What?" My explosive response echoed in the stillness.

"Indigestion. At least, that's their best guess. Her doctors couldn't find any problem. There's nothing wrong with her heart. In fact, it's amazingly strong for a woman her age. They only kept her overnight as a precaution. They're releasing her first thing in the morning."

Along with relief came frustration. I'd made a harrowing six-hundred-mile trip, worried out of my mind the whole way, and had abandoned my investigation because my mother had heartburn.

"She won't admit it," Caroline said, "but after her stroke, she feels vulnerable."

I couldn't deny a nagging suspicion. Priscilla Skerritt was no more vulnerable than a barracuda. As manipulative as she'd been her entire life, she wouldn't hesitate to use trickery to bring me home. She was obsessed with my wedding and determined to have me dance to her tune. "You're sure she didn't fake this?"

Caroline looked shocked. "You're not serious?"

"You said she asked for me."

My sister nodded.

"When was the last time Mother wanted to see me without some ulterior motive?"

Caroline opened her mouth as if to protest, but, apparently struck by the truth of my reasoning, shrugged instead. "What do you think she wants?"

"The two of you have been driving me nuts with plans for a big wedding I want nothing to do with. She craves the spotlight as mother of the bride in the biggest wedding Pelican Bay has ever seen, her words, not mine. But I keep thwarting her goals. She didn't want me leaving town without finalizing those plans, so she's made sure I hurried home."

"That's a horrible thing to imply about your own mother."

"Then convince me I'm wrong. Give me one good reason why Mother wouldn't stoop to such a trick. You know her as well as anybody."

"Well—" Again Caroline hesitated.

I waited, wanting her to prove me wrong, fearful that she couldn't.

"You don't want a big wedding?" she finally said in the same tone she might have used to ask whether I really wanted both legs amputated.

I sighed. "That's what I've been trying to tell you for the last two months."

Caroline shook her head in disbelief. "It's all Mother's talked about."

"*Mother*, not me. And it's not going to happen."

She studied my face, recognized the sincerity of what I was saying and appeared to accept it. "She isn't going to be happy."

"Since when has Mother ever been happy where I'm concerned?"

"Oh, Margaret—" Caroline grabbed my hand and squeezed it, but, again, she couldn't deny the facts. "What are you going to do?"

"I'm begging you now to cease and desist all this wedding nonsense. And I'm going to tell her in no uncertain terms to back off."

"When?"

"As soon as she's had a few days to recover from her 'indigestion,' so I don't look like the heartless, ungrateful child she always claims me to be." And after I'd had time to cool my temper and gather my courage. "Go home, Caroline. Get some sleep. At this point, Mother's probably in better shape than you are."

I stood as Bill got off the elevator.

Caroline rose beside me and gave me a hug. "Thanks for coming all that way so fast. You have a good heart, Maggie."

I hugged her back. "Help me out here, Caro. Don't encourage Mother in her wedding plans."

Caroline released me. "If you're sure that's what you want."

Bill strode down the hall toward us. Without a word of complaint, he'd driven me all the way from South Carolina, provided moral support and still had the good humor to smile at almost midnight, even though he had to be exhausted.

God, I loved him, but I'd never be convinced I deserved him.

"Believe me, Caroline, not wanting a big wedding is one of the few things in life I *am* sure about."

Bill spent the night, what little was left of it, at my condo, and the next morning I drove him to the marina for a change of clothes and to pick up his car before I went to the office.

Roger greeted me in the reception area with yelps of joy and began whirling like a dervish, but still managed to create enough forward momentum to follow me into my office.

Darcy displayed more reserve. "Back early?"

"Long and frustrating story," I said. "Any messages?"

She shook her head. "Everything's been quiet. But I did check on assistance for those elderly sisters Bill told me about."

I drew a blank before remembering Bessie Lassiter from the Historical Society whose shoplifting record Bill had uncovered. "Find anything?"

"I got them on the waiting list for Meals on Wheels. Deliveries will start in a few weeks."

"Thanks. You're an angel."

Darcy grinned. "Not to hear my mama tell it."

I shook my head and grimaced. "Let's leave our mamas out of it this morning."

She raised her eyebrows but made no further comment. She was well aware of my ongoing difficulties with dear old mom. "I'm going downstairs for some tea," she said. "You want anything?"

"Coffee and pastry. Get some for Bill, too, please. He'll be here soon."

I put through a call to Terry Pender, who said she'd arrange for me to talk to Alicia at the jail later in the morning. When I hung up, Bill had arrived, and Darcy had returned with breakfast.

With Roger curled against his thigh, Bill sat on the sofa in my office, coffee in one hand, cruller in the other.

"I'll be interviewing Alicia again this morning," I told him. "I want to find out more about the relationship between Ashton and Celeste. Maybe Alicia saw or heard something."

Bill nodded. "I'll pay a visit to Keating. See if he'll share what he has on Celeste. We don't even know her real name."

"You going to tell him about Garcia?"

"Let's call Adler first. Find out where Garcia's living these days."

In the turmoil over Mother's pseudo-heart attack, I'd forgotten about having Adler check the Department of Motor Vehicles to see if Garcia had a Florida license. "I'll call Adler this afternoon."

I reached into my top desk drawer, removed a bottle of Benadryl, popped a capsule into my mouth and washed it down with coffee. I had hoped that the recent solving of the cold cases of child killers that had begun my allergy to murder sixteen years ago would have alleviated the hives that dealing with murder invariably produced. Unfortunately, I had developed a chronic condition with only one way to gain temporary relief: catch Willard Ashton's killer.

In the visitor's room at the county jail, Alicia Langston appeared less traumatized than the last time I'd seen her but also more pitiful. Dark smudges circled her eyes, as if she hadn't slept in days, and her prison clothes hung on her as if two sizes too big. She started at the slightest noise and almost jumped off her chair when the guard slammed the heavy door as he left us.

"Anything you need?" I asked.

She shook her head. "Ms. Pender's taking care of me. But I hate this place. How soon before I can go home?"

Maybe never if Bill and I didn't get a lucky break. "Are you practicing your meditation?"

I didn't subscribe to oneness with the Universal Spirit, but my father had been a great believer in the healing effects of meditation and prayer. If nothing else, the practice might keep the kid sane. I was certain her fellow inmates weren't women she'd otherwise have encountered in her sheltered, upper middle-class life. I doubted *their* tattoos were tastefully small butterflies or delicate blossoms in provocative places, and I was also certain that their vocabularies contained phrases Alicia had never heard or read in the USF library. In addition to being scared, Alicia was most likely in culture shock.

"I haven't felt like meditating." Her words came out in a whisper.

"Try it," I encouraged. "It'll help."

I tugged a copy of the sketch of Jorges Garcia from my pocket, unfolded it and passed it across the table. "Have you ever seen this man?"

Alicia studied the sketch for a moment, then shook her head.

"You never saw him at Grove Spirit House?"

Again she shook her head. "I'd remember. He's kinda scary looking with that scar on his cheek." Her eyes widened. "You think he killed The Teacher?"

"We're checking him out. Garth saw him in the compound the night before the murder. Did you see or hear anything unusual that night?"

She closed her eyes for a moment, as if trying to remember, then opened them. "I slept in a tiki hut on the other side of the compound from the others. I didn't hear anything out of the ordinary, but I did see lights on late in the dining hall."

"Somebody getting a midnight snack?"

"I didn't see anyone, just lights."

Whoever had been in the dining hall had probably planted the belladonna in the refrigerator. Either Garth had surprised Garcia as he was leaving the dining hall, or Garcia had encountered Garth. Or Celeste had paid the kitchen a visit of her own.

"Has Garth been to see you?" I asked.

She blushed. "Every day. He's been wonderful."

"He's not angry? You jilted him and took his money. If it were me, I'd be pissed."

"Garth's not like that. He's worried sick about me. He wants to go through with the wedding—if you and Ms. Pender can get me out of here in time."

Don't hold your breath, kid. Out loud I said, "He's very forgiving."

"Garth's a good guy. Always has been."

"So why'd you leave him?"

Alicia flushed even deeper and picked at the cuticle on her left thumb. "I was stupid. The Teacher was feeding me a line, the same line he's used on dozens of women, according to Ms. Pender, and I fell for it."

"Don't beat yourself up over it. Ashton was good at his con. He preyed on women who were too trusting."

She looked me straight in the eye. "Somebody didn't trust him."

"Celeste, maybe?"

Alicia thought for a moment. "They had a strange relationship. Part of the time, they operated totally in sync, as if each knew what the other was thinking. At other times, antagonism sparked in the air between them."

"You ever hear them quarrel?"

"Two nights before he died, I heard angry voices coming from their quarters."

"Any idea what they were fighting about?"

"I couldn't make out the words." She flashed a rueful smile. "I was so stupid. I thought they were fighting about me."

"You?"

"I thought The Teacher was in love with me and that Celeste was jealous." She shivered in the air-conditioning, pumping stale prison air from the vent behind her, and hugged herself, as if trying to keep warm.

"You thought he was in love with you? But you don't think so now?"

Her expression turned sad. "He didn't care about me. All he wanted was my money. So why would he and Celeste have fought over me?"

Her question was rhetorical, so I didn't try to answer it. Married couples often quarreled, but, fortunately, seldom did such disagreements result in one offing the other. Was the Ashtons' case the exception, or had someone other than Celeste done the deed? My investigation was going in circles, and Alicia was counting on me to get her out in time for her wedding in three weeks.

Maggie Skerritt, supersleuth. No sweat.

I folded the sketch of Garcia and returned it to my pocket. "If you think of anything else that might be helpful, call Ms. Pender."

The guard came in to return Alicia to her cell, and I left the jail, wondering if the poor kid would ever walk down any aisle but that of a state prison.

CHAPTER 17

Over a late lunch in our booth at the Dock of the Bay, I gave Bill an account of my visit with Alicia. On the Wurlitzer in the bar, Toby Keith was belting out "I Ain't As Good As I Once Was," and I was feeling the same. The facts in this case weren't clicking together to form a pattern that I could follow to lead me to Ashton's killer. None of the puzzle pieces fit.

After I'd summed up what Alicia had told me, I asked, "Any luck with Keating?"

"Not at first." Bill squeezed a slice of lime into his Corona. "But when I offered to take him deep sea fishing on the *Ten-Ninety-Eight,* he loosened up."

I shook my head in mock disapproval. "Bribing an officer. That's a felony."

"Spending a day on the water with this guy will be punishment enough. He has an ego the size of Australia." Bill's scowl cleared and his blue eyes danced with amusement. "But at least he has good taste in women."

"You talked about women?" I guessed it was a guy thing.

Bill shook his head. "Not just any woman. We talked about you. Keating wanted to know what working with you is like. You apparently interest him."

I almost choked on my iced tea. "He's young enough to be my—"

"Brother. When are you going to face it, Margaret? You don't look a day over thirty-five. And you're hot."

The look he gave me was spiking my temperature. "Those are hot flashes. Either that, or my inner child, playing with matches."

I gulped more tea to cool things down and changed the subject. "So what did you learn about Celeste?"

"Her real name is Rebecca Franklin, originally from Cleveland."

"Any priors?"

He shook his head. "Her record's clean. But here's an interesting tidbit. Her mother's dead."

"The one Hector Morales said she was visiting every week before her husband died?"

Bill grinned. "I love it when that happens. So I asked Keating if he had phone logs for Grove Spirit House."

"Did he?

"Not only that, he showed them to me. He's so certain Alicia's his killer, he's not paying attention to the other evidence."

The satisfaction on Bill's face promised more to come. "Which is?" I prodded.

"Dozens of calls to Gerald Shively in Fort White over the entire time the Ashtons have had their Pelican Bay number."

Interesting. Those elusive puzzle pieces were moving closer together. "Too bad there's no way to know whether Ashton or Celeste placed the calls."

"All of the calls were at least fifteen minutes in duration, most longer. If Shively was as furious with Ashton as he implied, I doubt they indulged in prolonged chats."

I thought for a moment. "Unless Shively was lying about the reason for his fight with Ashton. Maybe Shively was a partner in the scam and killed Ashton because he stiffed him on the profits."

Bill shook his head. "I'm not buying the long conversations. Guys with their kind of history don't have much to say to each other. A few threats, a few curses, and the phone calls are over."

I grinned. "The old F-you, strong letter to follow?"

"Exactly. You talked to Adler yet?"

"I'll call him when we get back to the office."

"Tell him I checked with Mackley, and that Abe's on for the Burns-Baker reception. I'll call Antonio to let him know we'll be working his security detail." Bill signed the credit slip, left a tip and slid from the bench. "I need to stop by the boat. Then I'll meet you at the office."

Darcy greeted me upon my return with the three most dreaded words in the English language. "Your mother called."

"Thanks," I said and immediately thought of a way to delay the inevitable. I went to my desk and called Adler at the Clearwater PD. "You in the middle of something?" I asked.

"Just having a snack."

I should have known. The only time Adler didn't eat was when he was asleep. But I couldn't be certain. Since a new disorder called *sleep eating* had been reported recently, the guy probably stuffed his face even then. "I need another favor, if you have the time."

"What's up?"

"I want an address for Jorges Garcia. Can you check the DMV database?"

"Hang on," he said around a mouthful of whatever he was consuming. Something delicious and fattening, knowing Adler.

Over the line, I could hear the creak of his chair and the click of his keyboard, then a quick intake of breath.

"Jesus, Maggie, there are hundreds of Jorges Garcias in the system."

"Check their photos. I'm looking for a bald guy with a scar across his right cheek."

"This may take a while. How soon you need it?"

Yesterday. "Whenever you have time to spare. Just call me if you find something, okay?"

"Will do."

"And Adler?"

"Yeah?"

"What did you decide about the Burns-Baker security gig?"

"Can't pass up the extra bucks."

"Sharon's okay with it?"

"We're cool. Is Abe in?"

"He is."

"If you need a fifth, Ralph's willing to help." Ralph Porter was Adler's current partner.

"Safety in numbers," I said. "Sign him up."

I hung up to wait for Adler's call. My desk was clear, so I started for Bill's office, but he was on another line, and from the few snips I heard of his conversation, I could tell he was doing a background workup on Rebecca Franklin, Celeste's alter ego.

Without further excuses, I could no longer postpone what I'd been putting off all day. I patted Roger, on guard on his window bookcase against a sneak attack from Main Street, told him to be a good boy for Bill, and stopped by Darcy's desk.

"When Bill gets off the phone, tell him I'm at my mother's, but I'll be back soon."

If I survived. I put on my big-girl asbestos panties and headed out to face the dragon.

I'd told Caroline I'd wait a few days to break the news to Mother that the big wedding was off, but if I waited much longer, I'd lose my nerve altogether.

On the way to Mother's house, I recalled a conversation I'd had with a behavioral therapist I'd consulted about Roger's embarrassing humping habit.

"Don't scold him," she'd said. "Distract him with something more interesting."

The problem was the only item Roger found more interesting than an attractive lower limb was food. If I used treats as a distraction every time Roger turned amorous, the pooch would pork up to unhealthy levels.

Strange how the mind makes leaps and connections. The fact that my brain operated that way helped in detective work and, amazingly, provided an answer to my dilemma with Mother. In fact, the solution that came to me out of the blue was so perfect that, by the time I parked in front of Mother's house, I was downright cheerful.

But before I bearded the lioness in her den, I circled the house to the back door to visit Estelle and make certain my suspicions about mother's sudden illness had been accurate.

As soon as Estelle opened the back door, I was engulfed by the aroma of cookies baking, a wave of nostalgia and Estelle's bear hug.

"Miss Margaret, am I glad to see you. Your mama's

been madder'n a wet hen cause you haven't been to see her. I can't settle her to save my life."

"I've been out of town." I took my familiar chair at the kitchen table, and Estelle poured me a glass of milk and plied me with cookies, as if I were still eight years old and had just arrived from school. "Is Mother all right?"

She sat across from me and twined her dark fingers together on the tabletop. "Right as rain, especially now you're here."

"What happened yesterday?"

Estelle rolled her eyes. "Miz Skerritt was in her morning room, looking at bride magazines and brochures that Frenchwoman from New York left her. I took in her mid-morning tea, and she took a sip, calm as you please, set her cup down, and said for me to call Miss Caroline, that she was going to the hospital."

"She wasn't in pain?"

Estelle shook her head. "I asked her. Asked if she wanted an ambulance, but she said no, just Miss Caroline. At first, I was scared silly, till I realize there wasn't anything wrong with Miz Skerritt but the gleam of mischief in her eyes."

"So she wasn't ill?"

Estelle shushed me. "Not so loud. She thinks she's got everybody fooled, but I haven't worked for somebody for over fifty years without knowing when they're sick and when they're not." She leaned across the table and whispered, "I think she jus' wanted you to come home to plan your wedding. She hasn't talked about anything else for months."

I nodded. Estelle had confirmed my worst suspicions. "I'll talk to her and put a stop to this foolishness."

I started to rise, and Estelle caught my hand. "You are going to marry your Mr. Malcolm, aren't you?"

I squeezed her hand and released it. "You bet. Just not in the style my mother is anticipating. We want a small wedding, maybe just the two of us and a couple of witnesses. You know I've never been one for a lot of fuss."

"I can still bake you a cake, can't I?"

I pushed to my feet. "I'd be disappointed if you didn't. Now, where's Mother?"

"In the family room. She's probably through with her nap and watching *Oprah* by now."

I took a deep breath, squared my shoulders and went in search. I found Mother where Estelle said she'd be, seated on an overstuffed chaise longue in the family room. She clicked off the television with the remote as soon as I entered the room.

"Margaret, how kind of you to come back to check on your mother."

As if she'd given me a choice. "I want to talk with you. Is now a good time?"

She beamed with triumph. "For you, I have all the time in the world, dear."

"You sure you're feeling up to it?"

She apparently remembered then that she'd faked a heart attack to get me home, and, like an awkward thespian, clutched her chest. "The doctors assure me that I'll be all right."

I smiled with more wickedness than warmth and took the chair opposite her. She'd provided exactly the opening I needed.

"Your heart problem started me thinking."

"About your wedding?" Her eagerness was almost funny, but I sobered my expression.

"About you, Mother, and all the good you've done for others through your charities over the years."

"Why, Margaret, what a nice thing to say." Her eyes teared, and I felt a stab of guilt. Although I was buttering her up for the kill, my compliment was true.

Priscilla Skerritt had been a force for good, not only in Pelican Bay but throughout the state.

"And considering the good you've done," I continued before I lost my nerve, "and your recent heart spell, I think you should honor Daddy and celebrate your recovery by holding a fund-raising gala for the American Heart Association."

"A wonderful idea—" She shook her head. "But not now. We have a wedding to plan."

"Mother," I said in my firmest voice. "I don't want a big wedding. I don't even want a church wedding. Bill and I will probably elope."

"But—"

"That," I plunged ahead, "is why I think your time and skills could be put to much better use planning a Valentine's Day Ball. You could raise hundreds of thousands of dollars for a good cause. And you could be the Queen of Hearts."

What woman, faced with the choice, wouldn't choose Queen of Hearts over mother of the bride any day? I pushed home my point. "Besides, you're much too youthful to be the mother of a bride who's old enough to be a grandmother."

I could almost see her mind working, sorting

visions of flowers, caterers, ball gowns, publicity and public acclaim.

I fired off another shot. "You could have the party here, and you already have the Hilton ballroom booked in case of rain."

She faltered with a momentary glance at the bridal magazines spread on the tabletop beside her chair.

"And you can expand the number of guests," I added quickly, "since you don't have to worry about the size of a church."

"But your beautiful wedding?"

"It never was *my* wedding," I said gently. "You know me, Mother. That's not my style."

"No," she agreed instantly and with sadness, "it isn't."

I administered my coup de grâce. "Your Valentine ball would rival the Omelet Parties," the social event of the year in Upper Pinellas, which raised money for programs for the mentally challenged. "You'd establish a wonderful precedent."

"But what will people think when I don't throw you a proper wedding?" Mother's insecurities had raised their ugly heads.

"They'll be so dazzled by your gala, they won't give my marriage any thought at all."

I rose and gathered up the bridal magazines and bro-chures. "I'll get these out of your way. I know you have a million things to do to be ready by February."

I held my breath, waiting for her to protest. But she didn't. Her eyes had glazed, her mind already occupied with the details of her charity event.

I leaned forward and kissed her papery cheek. "Glad to see you looking so well, Mother, but I must get back to work."

She was reaching for the phone to call Caroline as I hurried to the kitchen to drop the wedding materials in the trash. I bit my tongue to keep from laughing out loud. When Roger misbehaved, I distracted him with a treat. I'd discovered that the same method worked on Mother. I made a mental note to send flowers and some chocolates to the doggy behavior therapist.

CHAPTER 18

"Any word from Adler?" I asked Bill when I returned to the office.

He shook his head. "Guess he's too covered up to sort through the photos for our man. But I found some interesting info on Rebecca Franklin, aka Celeste."

I settled into the chair across from his desk. "I'm listening."

"Celeste ran away from home at sixteen. She wanted to be a country music star, so she ended up in Nashville working as a waitress. Either she had no talent or no lucky breaks, because she never had a shot at becoming a singer. She did, however, hook up with Ryan Wayne, faked her age, and married him, just before he was sent to prison for a series of car thefts and burglaries."

"You can't say she didn't know what she was getting into."

I could never understand women so desperate to marry that they blindly committed to men like Ryan Wayne/Ashton, who were so obviously bad. My Bill was as good as they came, yet I was balking at dipping a toe into the matrimonial pool, much less taking the plunge.

"And if she was as frightened of him as Cynthia Woods implied," he said, "I can't understand why she stayed with him all those years."

"Abused women have had their heads messed with," I reminded him. "They begin to believe they're to blame for their troubles and that their abusers are mistreating them for their own good. Their abusers create a sense of dependency. And the feeling that there's nowhere for them to go, that no one else will put up with them, and they're too inadequate to look after themselves."

I recalled Celeste, standing in the gazebo in shock and wondering where she would go now that her husband was dead. "Celeste definitely fits the pattern."

"We'll know more when we talk to Garcia," Bill said, "and find out why he was at Grove Spirit House."

"In the meantime, I have a project for us."

Bill raised his eyebrows. "What kind of project?"

"Remember Bessie Lassiter, the elderly shoplifter from the Historical Society?"

He nodded.

"Darcy's arranged for Meals on Wheels for her and her sister, but they won't start for a few weeks. So while I was at Mother's this afternoon, I had Estelle make up a shopping list. I thought we could put together a basket of staples and other goodies and take it to them to tide them over."

"It's a good idea." Bill's smile dropped to a frown. "But I doubt they'll go for it. Bessie's a very proud woman. She won't like charity."

"Then we'll tell her she won the grand prize in the drawing we had to celebrate the opening of our business."

"We've been open for months. You think they'll fall for that?"

"Turn on your charm," I said, "and they'll never know what hit them."

Minutes later, Bill dropped me off at Publix and drove off toward Pier 1 to find a suitably large basket. I hated grocery shopping, but if I had to do it, Publix was the place. The only problem was that in their upgrades of their facilities, the company had created mega-buildings. The Pelican Bay store was so huge, if I bought green bananas in the produce section at one end, the fruit was ripe by the time I finally reached the other end and was ready to check out.

Dodging elderly couples shopping hand-in-hand and mothers with fidgety children in their baskets or trailing alongside, I filled my cart with muffins and a pie from the bakery, fresh fruits and vegetables, and boxes of pastas. I added a variety of canned goods and paper products, and topped the cart off with a bouquet from the floral section and a gift certificate that the Lassiter sisters could use to purchase meat or frozen entrées. I didn't like to cook, but I loved to eat, so I figured I'd done all right.

Bill was waiting in the parking lot when I came out, and we transferred the items from the bags in my cart into the oversize basket he'd stowed in the rear of his SUV.

"Looks good enough to eat," Bill said.

Even though we'd had a late lunch, my stomach growled in agreement.

"This should keep them well-fed until their Meals on Wheels begin," Bill added with a nod of satisfaction and slammed the hatch.

The drive to the Lassiter sisters' tiny home on Tangerine Street was a short one. The house was in an older section of town on a street that paralleled the Pinellas Trail, an old railroad bed that had been converted into a linear park that ran the length of the county. The neighborhood, desirable because of its proximity to the waterfront, had been undergoing a revitalization as new families moved in. Many of the houses sported large additions and exterior remodels that promised more of the same inside.

By comparison, the Lassiter place, a small square box built of concrete blocks and painted a fading pink, appeared stuck in a time warp. I doubted any changes had been made on the structure since it had been built in the 1940s. The lawn was neatly trimmed, and shrubs and plants long out of style, such as Turk's cap, Surinam cherry, periwinkle and crown-of-thorns, filled the foundation beds. A melaleuca tree shaded the front jalousie windows from the sharp angle of the setting sun.

Bill parked in the empty driveway. There was no car in the carport, either, and I doubted the Lassiter sisters, even if capable of driving, could afford a vehicle or its insurance.

We climbed out of the SUV, and Bill had gone to the rear to retrieve the basket when a woman's high-pitched scream burst through the open windows.

"Look out," she cried, "he's coming your way."

Another ear-splitting shriek split the quietness.

"Keep away from me, you low-down snake," a second female voice shouted.

The thud of blows reverberated in the evening air, followed by a crash and the sound of breaking glass.

Bill and I exchanged glances, then darted toward the house. Another scream emanated from the rear. We raced through the carport to the large screen porch at the back of the house.

Visible through the screen, a very old woman, tall and gangly with her white hair coiled in braids atop her head, tottered on a low footstool. She clutched the skirt of her cotton housedress above her knees. Another elderly woman, shorter with her white hair cropped above her ears, was wielding a broom like a Samurai warrior, slashing and lunging at something in the far corner. The ceramic pieces from a broken lamp littered the floor among the wicker furniture.

"Don't kill it," the woman on the stool shouted. "Just get it out of here."

"I'm trying," her companion said, her voice wheezing with exertion, "but the danged fellow doesn't want to leave."

"Can we help?" Bill called.

"Open the door!" the broom wielder shouted.

Bill whipped open the screen. The tiny woman worked her broom over the floor like a hockey player moving a puck across the ice, and a four-foot black racer slithered ahead of her and out the door. Bill and I leaped out of its path.

"Whew!" The woman tossed aside the broom and collapsed into the nearest chair.

Bill hurried inside to help the other lady off her stool.

"Thank you, young man." She released his hand and smoothed her skirt. "You arrived in the nick of time. We hate snakes, but not enough to kill them, so they keep coming back."

Bill told the women our names. "We're with Pelican Bay Investigations."

"I'm Violet Lassiter," the tall one said, "and that's Bessie, my sister." Violet turned to her younger sister. "Are we being investigated, Bessie?"

Bessie, still catching her breath from her snake encounter, fanned her face with her hand. "I hope not.

I don't like trouble." She looked at Bill. "We've met, haven't we?"

"A few days ago. That must have been when you entered our drawing."

"You entered a drawing?" Violet asked Bessie. "For what?"

"I don't remember. But then I don't remember a lot of things these days." Bessie looked back at Bill. "But I do remember you, so if you say I entered, then I must have."

"You not only entered," I said, "you won."

"Not a trip to Vegas, I hope," Violet said with a frown, "with transportation not included. That's a rip-off."

"Nothing so grand as a trip," I said quickly. "Just one of the gift baskets we're giving away to celebrate our new business venture."

"It's in the car," Bill said. "I'll get it."

Violet sat in a folding aluminum chair with nylon webbing and waved toward an old-fashioned glider. "Have a seat."

I sat to wait for Bill's return.

"You really have to be more responsible, Bessie," Violet said. "You can't go around doing things you don't remember. You need to write them down."

Bessie straightened her spine and glared at her sister. "When are you going to stop treating me like a child? I'm eighty-four years old. You can at least give me credit for having lived long enough to have learned *something*."

"Hmmmph. You're still a baby compared to me. After all, I'm the one who got a personal letter from the president on my one-hundredth birthday."

"And you wouldn't have gotten that if I hadn't written and requested it," Bessie snapped back.

The way the sisters were bickering, Violet was lucky Bessie didn't come after *her* with the broom.

"You have a lovely place here," I said, hoping for a cease-fire.

"Folks in the neighborhood think it's an eyesore," Violet said.

"They don't!" Bessie protested.

"Of course they do. We're the only ones not spending money like water to renovate our property. They'd kick us out if they could."

Bessie shook her head and looked at me. "Our neighbors are very nice."

"They're pains in the butt," Violet corrected.

"Violet!"

Violet grinned at me. "One of the advantages of being my age is being able to say what I think."

"Just because you're old doesn't mean you're right," Bessie said.

Luckily, Bill returned with the basket before the sisters came to blows.

"Oh, my." Bessie clasped her hands together in delight.

"What's the catch?" Violet said.

"There is no catch," Bill assured her.

Violet eyed him with distrust. "We don't have to sign up for water softeners or some danged annuity or buy magazines?"

"All you have to do is enjoy." I handed her my card. "And if you ever have a problem you need solved, remember our agency is here to help."

"Thank you," Bessie said, "and don't mind Violet. She's too mouthy for her own good."

"Thank you," Violet said. "And please ignore my little sister's bad manners."

"You're very welcome," Bill said. "Enjoy."

He caught my eye, and we made a quick retreat with the women's voices following us to the car.

"Put those flowers in some water," Violet said.

"Just because you're the oldest doesn't give you the right to boss me around," Bessie countered.

"And stay out of those muffins. We'll have them for supper."

Bill was grinning as we drove away. "Makes their longevity all the more amazing, doesn't it? Not only that they apparently have their health, but that they haven't killed each other by now."

In spite of their bickering, I'd sensed the underlying affection between the two sisters. Caroline and I had never fought. We'd never been that close, I realized with regret.

CHAPTER 19

Adler didn't call back with the info on Jorges Garcia until late the next afternoon.

"Sorry to take so long," he said. "We've been working a homicide, a drive-by in the North Greenwood area."

"Gang activity?" I asked.

"Probably. There's been tension in the neighborhood, dueling graffiti."

"You be careful." I sounded like his mother. "Those drug-crazy kids shoot without thinking."

"Ralph is watching my back," he said with a smile in his voice, "almost as well as you used to."

Before I teared up with nostalgia, I asked, "What have you got on Garcia?"

"He lives just outside Fort White." Adler rattled off the address and I jotted it down. "He's your man all right. I compared his driver's license photo with his mug shot from his Tennessee prison days. Same guy, just older and uglier."

"Probably meaner, too."

"Yeah, you be careful yourself, Maggie."

"You've saved us a lot of legwork. Thanks."

I hung up and went into Bill's office. Like a tan shadow, Roger trotted behind me.

"Adler's located Garcia." I told Bill the address.

He smiled with satisfaction. "His proximity to Shively can't be a coincidence."

"Ready to check him out?"

Bill nodded. "But first we need a direct line to Keating. If something goes down, we have no authority to detain or arrest."

"I'll take care of it."

I returned to my desk and phoned the Pelican Bay substation.

"Garrett," I said in my sultriest voice when the detective came on the line. "It's Maggie Skerritt."

"Well, hel-lo." His enthusiasm was almost pathetic.

"I need a favor."

"Anything, as long as it's not illegal."

I laughed at his feeble joke. "Just a number where I can reach you night or day at a moment's notice."

I could hear his heavy breathing. "You thinking about taking me up on getting together?"

"Um...possibly." I let him draw his own conclusions.

"Then here's my cell number. You can reach me any time."

I wrote down the number on my desk pad. "Thanks."

"And Maggie..."

"Yes?"

"I'll be waiting."

Garrett knew I was engaged to Bill, but his super-sized ego made him think he was a contender.

"Believe me, Garrett, I hope I'll be calling you soon." I said in my best imitation of Marilyn Monroe and hung up.

With Keating's cell number tucked in my pocket, Roger once again in Darcy's care and Bill at the wheel of his monster machine, we struck out toward Fort White.

Unfortunately, it was quitting time, and everyone who lived in the northern suburbs and beyond and commuted to work was also headed in the same direction. Traffic slowed to a crawl, and by the time we hit the open stretches of U.S. 19 in Levy County, the sun was dropping like a rock.

Darkness had fallen when we arrived in Fort White and followed a secondary road east toward the interstate. Five miles out of town, we found the address Adler had given us. Built in the 1930s as an overnight stop for visitors driving south toward the beaches, the motor court, long too dilapidated for the tourist trade, had been rented out as low-income housing. Weeds sprouted in the asphalt of the drive that circled a swimming pool, empty except for piles of trash and old furniture. Lights streamed from the tiny cabins set back among the pines, and most had their doors and windows propped open in hopes of catching a breeze in the stifling humidity. Grown-ups, children and several large mongrel dogs spilled over from the crowded spaces onto the porches, in search of a breath of cooler air among the lingering odors of cooking.

We located Garcia's place at the far end of the semicircle. Bill's headlights swept across an aging Pontiac Firebird with oxidizing black paint parked beside the cabin. I started to get out when Bill did, but he stopped me with a hand on my arm.

"Let me handle this." He registered my look of

surprise in the glow of the dome light. "Garcia might respond more quickly to a man. And to a single interrogator."

I nodded. "I'll be watching."

Bill turned on the ignition long enough to lower the window on the passenger side. "You should be able to hear from here, too."

He stepped out and walked to the sliver of porch at the front of the cabin, but he didn't climb the stairs. "Hey, Jorges," he called through the open door, "can I talk to you, amigo?"

A short but muscular man stepped onto the threshold and turned on the porch light. He was dressed in a dirty white undershirt, jeans and motorcycle boots. Tattoos covered his skin from the top of his neck, down his chest and arms to his hands. His bald head gleamed beneath the feeble glow of the bare bulb, and at least one gold tooth glinted in the dim light. He held a machete in his right hand.

"I don't know you," he said in a cold voice.

"No, you don't. I'm Bill Malcolm with Pelican Bay Investigations." Bill flashed his ID, stepped up so Garcia could see it, handed Garcia his business card and stepped back.

"Why you investigating me, man?" Garcia asked in the same hard tone. "I done nothing."

"Of course not." Bill appeared at ease, but he moved farther away from Garcia, opening the distance.

Any good cop knew a man with a knife, especially with a big blade like Garcia's machete, could cover ground faster than the cop could draw his weapon if they were too close together. And Bill's SIG-Sauer was tucked in its holster beneath his Hawaiian shirt at his waist. I slid my gun from my purse and held it at the ready below the window, just in case.

"You may be a witness to something, however," Bill added from his safer distance.

"Witness to what?"

"We have a man who identified you at Grove Spirit House in Pelican Bay a few nights ago."

"Sí, I was there. So what?"

Garcia's quick admission surprised me. No excuses, no alibis. The guy acted as if he had nothing to hide.

"Why were you there?" Bill asked.

"No big deal." With his left hand, Garcia scratched his chest. "I went to pick up something."

"Mind telling me what?" Bill asked.

"Some jewelry, love letters, that kind of shit, for a

gringo in town. He was breaking up with his girlfriend. Wanted them back."

"Gerald Shively?"

"Sí, he's the one."

Bill pressed on. "You drove his truck."

For the first time, Garcia hesitated. "He loaned it to me." He hefted the machete. "Shively, he's not saying I stole it?"

"No, no one's accusing you of anything," Bill said quickly. "I'm here to ask if you saw anything suspicious that night?"

"Suspicious?"

"A man died at Grove Spirit House. He was murdered."

"*Mierda!* I know nothing of any murder. And I think you better leave now."

"You didn't see anyone else at the compound?"

"Just a tall, skinny kid with glasses. Maybe he is your killer." But there was no conviction in Garcia's voice. He knew more than he was telling, but the way his grip was tightening on the machete indicated he'd finished talking.

"Thanks for your help." Bill turned and headed for the car.

I kept my eye on Garcia, who remained on the porch, glaring at Bill with a scowl that wrinkled the scar on his cheek.

Bill slid onto the driver's seat, started the car and raised my window. "Which way to Shively's place?"

I pointed back toward town.

Bill pulled onto the highway and headed toward Fort White. He'd gone only a few hundred yards when he stopped, backed into a drive almost covered by underbrush and turned off the engine.

In a few minutes, Garcia's Firebird roared by in the direction of town. Bill waited until he was well past, then pulled onto the highway and followed him.

When Garcia turned south at the town's main intersection, I was sure he was headed for Shively's. Bill tailed him, far enough behind to avoid detection, and just as I'd expected, the Firebird made the turn into Shively's neighborhood.

Bill pulled to the shoulder of the highway and waited several minutes before following the Firebird into the riverside development. By then, Garcia had already disappeared onto Shively's street, so I had to give Bill directions. He killed his headlights and eased slowly down the road that lacked streetlights but was partially illuminated by intermittent security lamps on the adjoining properties. When we reached Shively's driveway, there was no sign of the Firebird parked on the street.

Bill drove past the entrance to Shively's drive, turned the SUV around and parked in the shadows of scrub oaks that overhung the street. We left the car and sprinted back to Shively's drive, then walked among the weeds on the shoulder to prevent the crunch of our feet on the crushed shells from announcing our presence.

I was thankful to be wearing jeans that protected my legs from thorns and scrapes, and I tried not to think about fleas, ticks and chiggers that could be crawling over my shoes and up my pant legs. I was already in a state of hyper-itching from overactive hives. I'd popped a Benadryl before leaving the car, but it had yet to take effect.

There was no moon, but light filtering through the trees from Shively's pole barn kept us on course and prevented us from tripping over anything. A screech owl called from a branch high above our heads, and something, probably a coon or possum, rustled in the brush off to our right. Beyond the house, something splashed in the waters of the river.

Ahead, a car door slammed violently, and Garcia's voice broke the stillness.

"Shively! Turn off that damned torch. We got to talk."

"Got nothing to say to you, Jorges," Shively shouted back.

"You got one choice, man. You talk or you die."

CHAPTER 20

Bill and I had edged as close to the pole barn as we could without being detected, and as loud as Garcia and Shively were shouting at each other, we could hear every word.

"You set me up, man," Garcia said.

"Cool it, Garcia. I have no idea what you're talking about."

"Just go in and pick up the stuff from the lady," Garcia chanted in a whiny, singsong voice. "No sweat, you said. In and out. You'd wait in the truck. Now I got an hombre asking questions about a murder."

Between the fronds of a saw palmetto, I could see the men beneath the lightbulbs strung across the ceiling of the pole barn. Garcia gripped his machete, but Shively hadn't shut down his torch. One move forward and Garcia was toast. Literally.

"I did wait in the truck," Shively said. "Besides,

I've looked up the newspaper reports of the murder on the Net. They've already arrested the killer."

Garcia didn't relax his hold on the hilt of his blade. "Then why is this man asking me questions?"

"You know how that works. You've been in the system. They want to convict this woman they say did it, and they have to dot their i's and cross their t's, so there's no grounds for appeal. So relax. That visit's probably the end of it."

"They visit you?" Garcia hadn't relaxed. His tone and body language remained tense and confrontational.

"No," Shively lied. "Why would they?"

"Maybe that skinny kid saw your license tag, and they traced it to you, and you sent them to me. I won't take the fall for this, man. I done my time and I ain't going back to jail. Not over some stupid lovers' quarrel."

"More likely," Shively said with cold dispassion, "the geek described you, not my truck. And when the police checked into Ryan Wayne's background, your prison fight popped up, mug shot, scarred cheek and all."

"Wayne's the hombre who died?" In his surprise, Garcia dropped the machete to his side.

"Poisoned by some little slut he was banging," Shively said.

"But, man, I got motive and I was there. They'll come after me."

"Not if you stay cool."

"They don't know I had no reason to kill him."

"He ripped your face."

"It's nada. A mark of honor, since I won the fight. I just wanted to make his life *destrado*, all the *venganza* for my face that I needed."

Shively's laugh was without warmth. "You made him plenty miserable with your anonymous complaints while he was here in Fort White. And when the local police broke up his operation, you had your revenge."

"*Sí*, so why would I want to kill him?"

"Like I said—" Shively's voice turned soothing, conciliatory "—the visit you had was just routine. They've got Wayne's killer, so you got nothing to worry about."

Shively had apparently succeeded in calming Garcia's fears. He loosened his hold on the machete. "All right, if you say so, man. But if they come after me, I'm giving you up."

Garcia stomped out of the pole barn, wrenched open his car door and got in. With a grinding of gears, he backed up the Firebird and stomped the accelerator, spewing crushed shell as he exited the drive. Bill and I ducked deeper into the underbrush to avoid exposure from his headlights.

As soon as Garcia left, Shively shut off his torch, pulled a cell phone from his pocket and punched in numbers.

"Answer the damned phone, Celeste," he muttered. After several rings, he flipped his phone shut and returned it to his pocket. He took a shirt from a peg, shrugged into it and headed for his truck, parked among the stilts that supported his house.

Bill and I made a run for the SUV. By the time Shively left his driveway, we were belted inside, ready to follow.

We tailed Shively to Chiefland, where he stopped to buy gas at a busy truck stop. Bill pulled into the far row of pumps and topped off his tank. I kept my face hidden beneath the brim of a ball cap I'd grabbed from the back seat. Shively, who obviously had other things on his mind, paid no attention to the surrounding vehicles. Bill fell in behind him again on U.S. 19 South when he left the gas station.

"You think Shively's our killer?" I asked Bill.

The discussion was moot, since we'd know more about Shively's motives when he reached Pelican Bay. Unless we were way off base, he was headed for Grove

Spirit House and Celeste. I was talking mainly to keep us from dozing off. The Benadryl had kicked in and alleviated my itching, but it was also threatening to put me to sleep.

"Celeste dumped him," Bill said. "Returned his gifts. Guys in love are often bitten by the stupid bug."

"What if Ashton's murder had nothing to do with Shively? Maybe Celeste wanted to get rid of her husband and deflect suspicion? She could lay the blame on Alicia or Shively and be home free."

Bill's forehead wrinkled in the glow of the dash lights. "You think she's that devious?"

"She was terrified of Ashton, Ryan, whatever his name du jour. Probably hated him. This was her chance for payback for his mistreatment and to finally get away."

Bill shrugged. "She looks like a black widow spider, so maybe she did devour her mate."

"I don't think Garcia's our man," I added.

"I agree. He was genuinely surprised by the turn of events."

"So that leaves Celeste and Shively," I said.

"Unless Garth Swinburn has us all fooled."

On an open stretch of highway, Bill eased off the gas to place more distance between us and Shively's truck, its taillights plainly visible ahead on the deserted highway.

"I hope not," I said. "Garth seems like a good kid, and Alicia's been through enough trauma without having her fiancé arrested."

I turned the radio up loud and Bill opened the windows in an effort to keep us alert.

When we left Hernando County and entered Pasco, I borrowed Bill's cell phone, removed Keating's number from my pocket and punched it in.

A sleepy voice answered.

"Hello, Garrett," I said in my breathy Marilyn Monroe voice. Or was it Jackie O? Both women had sounded like idiot bimbos, which was the effect I was going for.

"Maggie?" Keating asked in a stronger voice. "It's one o'clock in the morning."

"I want to see you."

"Yeah?" His eagerness was palpable. "Where?"

"The gazebo at Grove Spirit House. Can you meet me there in an hour?" I was counting on Shively having the same destination. If not, I'd call Keating with a change of venue.

"Why there?" he asked.

"It's secluded…and romantic. Where's your sense of adventure?"

"Sure," he agreed too readily.

"But don't let anyone see you. Stay hidden and I'll find you." I gave a throaty chuckle. "We'll make this our little game."

"In an hour, sweet cakes."

Sweet cakes? Eeewwww. Trying not to gag, I ended the call.

Bill was grinning at me.

"What?"

"God will get you for raising the poor man's hopes, along with…other things. How come you seldom use that sexy voice on me?"

"I couldn't tell Keating the real reason I want to see him. He's so convinced Alicia's guilty, he wouldn't have met me merely to pursue the Ashton case."

"Guess he's in for a surprise," Bill said with a laugh. His expression sobered suddenly. "You don't find Keating attractive, do you?"

"Jealous?"

"Should I be?"

"Quit talking like a cop." I leaned across the console and kissed his cheek. "It's sweet that you're jealous, but you have no cause for concern. I have no interest in Keating. Garcia, on the other hand..." I smacked my lips.

"Don't make me stop this car," Bill warned with fake seriousness.

"I love it when you talk tough."

"And I love you, Margaret." He reached over and squeezed my hand. "You seem so much happier now that you've laid down the law with your mother."

"No more wedding bell blues," I agreed.

Bill pulled his attention back to the road and the truck far ahead of us. "He's taking the exit on to 54. So far so good."

An hour later, Bill killed his headlights and pulled onto the shoulder of Hidden Lake Road, out of the range of the gate's surveillance camera. Shively's truck was parked in front of the closed gate, but Shively was nowhere to be seen.

A large dark sedan pulled up behind us. I hopped from the passenger seat and met Keating as he climbed from his car. Bill followed.

"What the hell is going on?" Keating asked in a loud, angry voice.

"Ssshhhh," I warned him. "We want your help."

I couldn't see Keating's face in the darkness, but I could hear the shock in his voice. "I don't do threesomes."

"Get your mind out of your jock strap," Bill said. "We're tracking Ashton's killer, and we need you to make the arrest."

"I've already made the arrest."

"And I'm betting you're wrong," I said. "Come with us and prove you're right."

Keating sighed. "What the hell. I'm awake, I'm dressed, and I'm here. What else am I going to do at two in the morning?"

"The gate's closed, so we'll have to go over the fence," Bill said.

"Me first." I grasped the chain link with Bill behind me. If anyone had to boost my butt, I wanted it to be him, not Keating.

I climbed the fence, swung one leg over the top, then the other, and dropped into the weeds below. Bill landed beside me, followed by Keating.

"Let's work our way back over to the drive," I whispered. "There's grass alongside and easier going."

In the moonless night, we didn't have to worry

about being spotted. I could barely make out the silhouettes of my two companions.

After a short tramp through the weeds in the grove, we reached the grassy strip that paralleled the drive and broke into a run. Behind me, Keating slipped on the dew-wet grass and went down with a muffled curse. Bill gave him a hand, and we continued in pursuit of Shively. We skidded to a halt at the flash of his light-colored shirt on the path heading toward the main pavilion. Its walls had been stacked back, open to the night, and dim light streamed from several groupings of lit candles. Celeste sat inside in a yoga position, open palms resting on her knees, eyes closed.

At Shively's approach, she opened them in alarm and leaped to her feet when he stomped up the stairs.

"What are you doing here?"

"Why'd you do it, Celeste?" he demanded.

"He gave me no choice." With a heartrending cry, Celeste plunged into Shively's arms like an actress in a perfume commercial, minus the slow motion. He clasped her close, as if never wanting to let go.

Concealed in the bushes, Keating, Bill and I listened. I waited for Celeste to confess to killing her husband and to explain to her lover why. And once Keating heard her, he'd have to release Alicia, and my job would be finished, hopefully before I contracted West Nile virus from mosquitoes the size of vampire bats that were feeding on my arms and neck. I resisted the urge to swat and focused my attention on the sweaty clench a few feet in front of me.

Finally, Celeste broke away and gazed up at Shively with tear-filled eyes. "The ring. Your letters. I gave them back because you demanded them. Don't you love me?"

I stifled a gag. Lovers' encounters, like the making

of sausages, were something I preferred not to witness. Unfortunately, for them and for me, in this case, I had no choice.

He cradled her face in his hands. "I hoped by forcing you to return them, you'd come to your senses. And come to me. But you didn't even call. Not even now that you're free. I don't understand."

"I didn't dare contact you." He released her and she wiped tears from her cheeks with the backs of her hands. "The police already suspect that I killed Ryan. If they find out about my affair with you, they'll have good reason to arrest me and let their other suspect go."

Beside me in the undergrowth, Keating uttered a soft grunt. I took his visceral reaction as an indication that he'd opened his mind to the possibility that he'd arrested the wrong woman. Or maybe his legs were cramping from crouching in the bushes.

"But I didn't kill Ryan," Celeste insisted. "I swear on my mother's grave."

Shively turned away, walked to the edge of the steps and sat on the top tread with his head in his hands.

"He'd found out about us," Celeste continued. "The night before you sent Garcia to pick up the things you'd given me. We had a terrible quarrel. I thought he was going to kill me, he was so angry. Probably the only reason he didn't was my promise that it was over and I was returning your gifts and would never see you again. He was so out of control, I was afraid he might come after you, too, if I didn't convince him that I meant what I said. But you have to believe me. I didn't kill him. The Langston woman must have done it."

Celeste's plaintive voice echoed on the night air, and I was getting nervous. If Celeste maintained her innocence, Alicia was out of options. Her only hope would be for Terry Pender to use Celeste's affair with Shively to raise reasonable doubt among the jury.

"It wasn't her," Shively mumbled through his fingers that still hid his face, and I couldn't tell if his words were a statement or a question.

Celeste folded herself onto the step beside him. "Was it Garcia? He's hated Ryan since their prison days. Did Garcia leave the poison in the kitchen after I returned your ring and letters to him?"

Shively's moan of anguish split the stillness. "It wasn't Garcia."

Beside him, Celeste tensed. "Then who?"

Shively dropped his hands and looked at her. "You still love Ryan, don't you?"

"How can you say that? The man was a monster."

"You could have left him any of those weekends you spent with me. All you had to do was stay in Fort White and never return. He wouldn't have known where to find you."

Celeste shook her head. "I needed time."

"You still loved him."

"No, I needed time to prepare. I'd been moving money from our joint account into an account under my real name for the last two years, but I had to do it in small enough increments that Ryan wouldn't be suspicious."

"I would have taken care of you."

She shook her head. "I swore that I would never be dependent on any man ever again. Not even one I love as much as you."

He groaned, shoved to his feet and paced the floor behind her. "God, I've botched everything."

Her gaze followed him back and forth across the room. "What are you saying?"

"I didn't mean to kill him."

She uttered a strangled cry. "Oh, God, Gerald, tell me it wasn't you. Please!"

Keating's swift intake of breath was loud enough to

give us away, but the couple was too wrapped up in their own emotions to notice.

Shively returned to sit next to Celeste and buried his face again, as if unable to look at her. "I didn't mean to kill him. You have to believe me."

"You were here that night?"

He sat for several minutes without saying anything. When he finally spoke, his voice was dead, without inflection, eerily similar to Celeste's tone when I'd talked with her the day after her husband had died.

"I put the deadly nightshade in the food in the refrigerator and freezer," he admitted, "while you were meeting Garcia at the gazebo."

"You could have killed me, too." Horror edged her words. "Did you even think of that?"

He lifted his head, smiled and shook his head. "Not you. You eat like a bird, you hate peas and anything green, so I knew you'd never consume enough of the berries or leaves to harm you." His smile vanished. "But I hadn't expected Ryan to die. I'd hoped the poison would send him to the hospital, long enough for you to make your escape and come to me."

"Ryan was a glutton," Celeste said. "He ate enough

of that pasta dish for six people, and it killed him. God, *you* killed him."

"I only wanted to make him sick enough to give you an opportunity to get away," Shively insisted. "Even though you were returning the gifts I'd given you, I suspected you were doing so under duress. I wanted to give you…us a chance."

Celeste began to cry again.

"You believe me, don't you?" Shively said. "I kept waiting for you to arrive at my place, or at least to call to say you were on the way. I didn't even know Ryan had died until some private eye showed up asking questions."

Celeste's tears stopped. "What?"

Shively nodded. "Some woman named Skerritt. But she was looking for Garcia. She didn't suspect anything."

"Did she find Garcia?"

Shively squirmed beneath her gaze. "Yes, but—"

"You idiot! Did he tell her about us?"

"Some guy from her agency came to see Garcia. Garcia told him you and I were finished and that he'd come here to pick up the gifts I'd given you."

Celeste shook her head. "They know about us now. It's only a matter of time before they piece it all together."

"More quickly than you'd think." Keating stood and stepped from the bushes. Bill and I followed.

Celeste and Shively looked up with a mixture of surprise and alarm.

"I heard everything," Keating said. "Gerald Shively, you're under arrest for the murder of Willard Ashton."

I had to give Keating credit. He'd taken the lazy way out by arresting Alicia in the first place, but when you beat him over the head with incontrovertible evidence, he sprang into action like a whirlwind.

Keating cuffed Shively and read him his rights. As the detective led Shively down the drive toward his car, Celeste watched, dry-eyed and hostile.

I couldn't help feeling sorry for her. "Will you be all right? Is there someone I can call to be with you?"

Her anger spilled over on me. "This is all your fault, bitch. Why couldn't you leave well enough alone?"

"Because I don't believe in allowing an innocent woman to pay for someone else's mistakes." My sympathy had evaporated, especially when I thought of all the people Celeste and Ashton had scammed. "Think of it as my way of achieving oneness with the Universal Spirit. Or you can call it cosmic justice, if you like."

Bill and I followed Keating and Shively up the

drive toward our cars. Watching the suspect, his hands bound behind him, I couldn't help wondering what kind of a man Shively had been before encountering Ashton and Celeste. Had he been basically good until his association with them had tainted his soul, their fraudulent retreat the tipping point in calling forth the evil that lurks in each of us? Or had something dark and malevolent in his spirit responded to the same characteristics in theirs?

Or maybe the whole fiasco was as Bill had suggested, merely a man in love being bitten by the stupid bug.

"You okay?" Bill asked when he opened the door of the SUV for me.

Before climbing in, I kissed him. "I'm fine."

I thanked my lucky stars. I never had to wonder about Bill. His intrinsic goodness was a given.

CHAPTER 22

The next morning, I was at my desk when Darcy and Roger arrived a few minutes before eight. She took one look at me and frowned. "What truck hit you, girl?"

"Didn't get any sleep," I said. "I've just come from the sheriff's substation. Bill and I caught Ashton's killer, and we had to give statements."

"Was it the wife?"

I shook my head. "The man she was having an affair with."

Darcy put her hands on her hips and shook her head. "Does love always make people stupid?"

I shrugged. "Sometimes I wonder."

"You want coffee or are you intending to get some sleep?"

"Coffee, please, if you're going to the bookstore."

"Bill, too?"

"He's gone back to the boat to get some rest."

"Good to know at least one of my employers has some sense."

She flounced out of the office and I reached for the phone. Terry Pender answered her cell phone immediately.

"You can arrange for your client's release," I told her. "Keating has the murderer and a confession."

"Not Garth Swinburn?"

"Nope, Gerald Shively, Celeste's secret squeeze."

"Thank God. Any more trauma, and Alicia would lose it for sure."

"Now all she has to worry about is her wedding," I said. Better her than me.

"You're good, Maggie, you and Malcolm. But that's why I hired you."

"Glad to be of service. Give my best to Alicia."

"I'm sure she'll be contacting you to thank you herself."

Terry hung up, and I scooped Roger into my arms. I'd missed the pooch. He licked my face briefly before squirming to be released. Hopping onto his bookcase, he assumed his surveillance of Main Street, on guard against vicious sanitation and UPS trucks.

I called Adler to let him know our case was closed and to thank him for his help.

"Already heard the news," Adler said. "Keating is taking full credit for the collar. Claims he knew all along Alicia wasn't guilty, but he wanted to throw the real killer off guard until he could nail him."

"No problem, as long as the true culprit's in jail and our client is free. Any luck on your drive-by case?"

"Some promising leads. Gotta go. See you at the Burns-Baker bash."

I hung up, exhausted but serene. Alicia Langston was free; my mother and sister were off my back; and Bill and I had made life a bit easier for the Lassiter sisters. Life was good. I removed the box of Benadryl from my purse and shoved it into the back of my top desk drawer.

I should have known the calm wouldn't last.

Two weeks later, I stood with Antonio in the rear of the upstairs banquet hall at Sophia's, waiting for the other shoe to drop. So far, the Burns-Baker reception had progressed in typical fashion. The newly married couple had been piped into the roomful of guests upon their arrival by bagpipes played by the Dunedin City Pipe

Band. Then the deejay had taken over. To the strains of Shania Twain's "From this Moment," Linda and Kevin danced their first dance as man and wife.

Kevin Baker looked strained, his smile tight, his body language tense, but I credited his discomfort to the hoopla of the event. Girls, present company excluded, dreamed of a fancy wedding, expensive bridal gowns, mountains of flowers and being queen for a day. Guys probably wished for a magic wand to make the whole ordeal go away so they could have a beer, kick back in their recliners and watch the latest sportscast.

Kevin's bride, on the other hand, looked radiant. Triumphant, even, since her smile had a touch of smirk. After dancing with her father to "Sunrise, Sunset," from *Fiddler on the Roof*, she retreated to the head table to watch Kevin and his mother circle the dance floor to "You Are the Sunshine of My Life."

The song ended and Kevin took his seat beside his new bride. The best man and maid of honor, then the newlyweds' respective parents flanked the couple.

Bill and Adler blended unobtrusively with the waitstaff behind the head table, and Ralph Porter and Abe Mackley did the same on opposite sides of the large hall.

Disguised as events coordinator in my floral dress

and Torquemada high heels, I shifted from one foot to the other as the familiar ritual unfolded without incident. After the bridal dinner had been devoured, the newlyweds cut the cake and fed each other a slice, resisting the fashionable but tacky trend of smearing each other's face with the dessert.

Beside me, Antonio breathed a sigh of relief. "Everything is going well, no?"

I nodded. "Everyone's having a great time. The parents and siblings have buried the hatchet, for tonight at least. Looks like your fears were unfounded."

"Ah, but better to be prepared than surprised."

At that moment, Kevin stood, grabbed a chair and carried it to the middle of the dance floor. With the expression of a man going to his execution, he seated his bride, removed her garter to a chorus of ribald comments and tossed the lacy wisp to his best man. Linda's smile faltered as she observed the grim set of her new husband's face.

Once the best man had the garter in hand, Kevin pointed to the deejay, who cued a drumroll, and Kevin held up his hands for silence. Kevin's sisters in their plum bridesmaid gowns rose from their seats and removed baskets from beneath the draped table.

Each basket was loaded with identical small flat packages, wrapped in white tissue paper and tied with black ribbons.

"Before my blushing bride tosses her bouquet," Kevin said, smiling now, "I have a present for each of you. Since the presents are identical and intended as a surprise, I ask that you wait until each guest has a package before you open yours."

Murmurs of speculation and appreciation sounded among the guests. The Baker sisters quickly distributed a gift to each guest, including the parents at the head table. Mrs. Baker beamed at her children. She might not have liked Kevin's choice for a bride, but she was unquestionably proud of her offspring. Mrs. Burns, on the other hand, was three sheets to the wind and downing another glass of champagne.

"Do you all have a gift?" Kevin asked.

"Yes!" the crowd responded with the enthusiasm of the festive and well-liquored.

"Then open," Kevin called.

Antonio and I had inched toward the table closest to us to look over the shoulders of the guests as they stripped the wrappings off their gifts.

A collective gasp went up across the room. At the

head table, Mrs. Baker fainted, and Mrs. Burns swore like a sailor.

The gifts were identical photographs of Linda Burns and the best man, sprawled in flagrante delicto across the tousled sheets of a queen bed in a room that was obviously a motel.

"As you can see," Kevin announced in the hush that had descended on the room, "my lovely bride has the morals of a slut. And my best man had no qualms about screwing his best friend's fiancée." He turned to Linda, who stood open-mouthed, her bouquet dangling from her fingers. "My attorney will contact you in the morning to annul this fiasco."

Before anyone could react, Kevin turned on his heel and strode out of the banquet room, throwing open the double doors until they banged against the wall and making his exit with panache.

I caught Bill's eye, and he nodded.

"Oh my God," Antonio groaned.

"Time for plan B," I assured him and, in concert with Bill, Adler, Ralph and Abe, swung into action as all hell broke loose.

Two hours later, Bill and I sat on the rear deck of the *Ten-Ninety-Eight*, drinks in hand, Roger curled in my lap.

"That went well," Bill said.

"Unless you were Linda Burns." Her wedding, as her mother had unwittingly predicted, had gone off without a "hitch."

"I'd say she had it coming."

"What I can't figure," I said, "is why Kevin went through the motions of a wedding when he was planning all along to have the marriage annulled."

Bill chuckled. "The photos were the knife in the back. The bride's family having to pay for the wedding and reception was the final twist. Not only was Linda humiliated in front of her family and friends, her parents are out several thousand dollars they wouldn't otherwise have spent."

"At least Antonio's happy. He has his banquet fee and his ballroom still intact."

Bill sipped his beer. "I hate to think what would have happened if we hadn't been there."

But we had been there, and our contingency plan had worked smoothly. Bill and Adler had whisked the Baker family into Bill's SUV and driven them off, stopping by the emergency room to have Mrs. Baker checked by a doctor after her fainting spell before depositing them at Kevin's apartment. Bill had suggested they spend the night there to give the Burnses time to cool down. And sober up.

Abe and Ralph had corralled the Burnses into the limousine, which was supposed to have taken the happy couple to the airport for their honeymoon but instead drove the entire family to their house on Pineland Circle.

At Sophia's, Antonio had offered the remaining guests drinks on the house; the deejay had cued up some happy tunes, and I'd stayed to supervise in case someone decided to get rowdy.

Bill laughed out loud.

"What's so funny?"

"Those two families still have to live next to each other."

"Maybe this will convince one of them to move."

"Or escalate the warfare."

"Not our problem," I said with satisfaction. "The sheriff's finest can deal with the Burns-Baker feud from now on."

Bill reached over and took my hand. "I'm glad we're not having a big wedding."

"You're sure?"

"Absolutely. Something quiet and intimate suits us better."

I squeezed his hand. In spite of the fiasco I'd witnessed at Sophia's, my attitude toward marriage had mellowed. The prospect of exchanging vows with Bill brought waves of pleasure instead of a cold sweat.

"Maybe we shouldn't wait until Valentine's Day," I said and meant it.

Bill tried but couldn't quite cover his surprise. "When did you have in mind?"

"Let's get the house furnished first," I said. "Then as soon as we're married, we'll have a gathering there for our closest friends."

"And your mother?"

"I'll suggest she hold a small reception at the Yacht Club for her friends. That will please her. Any objections?"

In the glow of the marina lights, he flashed his crooked smile. "Can I get this in writing?"

"You afraid I'll lose my nerve?"

"You have expressed reservations in the past," he reminded me.

I placed Roger atop a cushion on the deck, slid onto Bill's lap and draped my arms around his neck.

"All gone," I said, "and—"

I was going to explain further, but the impact of his kiss derailed my train of thought.

* * * * *

Be sure to pick up the next Maggie Skerritt mystery by USA TODAY *bestselling author Charlotte Douglas, coming in 2007!*

"Now that's the kind of man you should be looking for," my mother, the self-appointed keeper of my shelf-life stamp, says. She points with her fork at a man in the corner of the Steak-Out Restaurant, a dive I've just been hired to redecorate. Making this restaurant look four-star will be hard, but not half as hard as getting through lunch without strangling the woman across the table from me. "*He* would make a good husband."

"Oh, you can tell that from across the room?" I ask, wondering how it is she can forget that when we had trouble getting rid of my last husband, she shot him. "Besides being ten minutes away from death if he actually eats all that steak, he's twenty years too old for me and—shallow woman that I am—twenty pounds too heavy. Besides, I am *so* not looking for another husband here. I'm looking to design a new image for this place, looking for some sense of ambience, some feeling, something I can build a proposal on for them."

My mother studies the man in the corner, tilting her head, the better to gauge his age, I suppose. I think she's grimacing, but with all the Botox and Restylane injected into that face, it's hard to tell. She takes another bite of her steak salad, chews slowly so that I don't miss the fact that the steak is a poor cut and tougher than it should be. "You're concentrating on the wrong kind of proposal," she says finally. "Just look at this place, Teddi. It's a dive. There are hardly any other diners. What does *that* tell you about the food?"

"That they cater to a dinner crowd and it's lunchtime," I tell her.

I don't know what I was thinking bringing her here

with me. I suppose I thought it would be better than eating alone. There really are days when my common sense goes on vacation. Clearly, this is one of them. I mean, really, did I not resolve less than three weeks ago that I would not let my mother get to me anymore?

What good are New Year's resolutions, anyway?

Mario approaches the man's table and my mother studies him while they converse. Eventually Mario leaves the table with a huff, after which the diner glances up and meets my mother's gaze. I think she's smiling at him. That or she's got indigestion. They size each other up.

I concentrate on making sketches in my notebook and try to ignore the fact that my mother is flirting. At nearly seventy, she's developed an unhealthy interest in members of the opposite sex to whom she isn't married.

According to my father, who has broken the TMI rule and given me Too Much Information, she has no interest in sex with him. Better, I suppose, to be clued in on what they aren't doing in the bedroom than have to hear what they might be doing.

"He's not so old," my mother says, noticing that I have barely touched the Chinese chicken salad she warned me not to get. "He's got about as many years on you as you have on your little cop friend."

She does this to make me crazy. I know it, but it works all the same. "Drew Scoones is not my little 'friend.' He's a detective with whom I—"

"Screwed around," my mother says. I must look shocked, because my mother laughs at me and asks if I think she doesn't know the "lingo."

What I thought she didn't know was that Drew and I actually tangled in the sheets. And, since it's possible she's just fishing, I sidestep the issue and tell her that Drew is just a couple of years younger than me and that I don't need reminding. I dig into my salad with renewed vigor, determined to show my mother that Chinese chicken salad in a steak place was not the stupid choice it's proving to be.

After a few more minutes of my picking at the wilted leaves on my plate, the man my mother has me nearly engaged to pays his bill and heads past us toward the back of the restaurant. I watch my mother take in his shoes, his suit and the diamond pinkie ring that seems to be cutting off the circulation in his little finger.

"Such nice hands," she says after the man is out of sight. "Manicured." She and I both stare at my hands. I have two popped acrylics that are being held on at weird angles by bandages. My cuticles are ragged and there's marker decorating my right hand from measuring carelessly when I did a drawing for a customer.

Twenty minutes later she's disappointed that he managed to leave the restaurant without our noticing. He will join the list of the ones I let get away. I will hear about him twenty years from now when—according to my mother—my children will be grown and I will still be single, living pathetically alone with several dogs and cats.

After my ex, that sounds good to me.

The waitress tells us that our meal has been taken care of by the management and, after thanking Mario, the owner, complimenting him on the wonderful meal and assuring him that once I have redecorated his place people will be flocking here in droves (I actually use those words and ignore my mother when she rolls her eyes), my mother and I head for the restroom.

My father—unfortunately not with us today—has the patience of a saint. He got it over the years of living with my mother. She, perhaps as a result, figures he has the patience for both of them, and feels justified having none. For her, no rules apply, and a little thing like a picture of a man on the door to a public restroom is certainly no barrier to using the john. In all fairness, it does seem silly to stand and wait for the ladies' room if no one is using the men's room.

Still, it's the idea that rules don't apply to her, signs don't apply to her, conventions don't apply to her. She knocks on the door to the men's room. When no one answers she gestures to me to go in ahead. I tell her that I can certainly wait for the ladies' room to be free and she shrugs and goes in herself.

Not a minute later there is a bloodcurdling scream from behind the men's room door.

"Mom!" I yell. "Are you all right?"

Mario comes running over, the waitress on his heels. Two customers head our way while my mother continues to scream.

I try the door, but it is locked. I yell for her to open it and she fumbles with the knob. When she finally manages to unlock and open it, she is white behind her two streaks of blush, but she is on her feet and appears shaken but not stirred.

"What happened?" I ask her. So do Mario and the

waitress and the few customers who have migrated to the back of the place.

She points toward the bathroom and I go in, thinking it serves her right for using the men's room. But I see nothing amiss.

She gestures toward the stall, and, like any self-respecting and suspicious woman, I poke the door open with one finger, expecting the worst.

What I find is worse than the worst.

The husband my mother picked out for me is sitting on the toilet. His pants are puddled around his ankles, his hands are hanging at his sides. Pinned to his chest is some sort of Health Department certificate.

Oh, and there is a large, round, bloodless bullet hole between his eyes.

Four Nassau County police officers are securing the area, waiting for the detectives and crime scene personnel to show up. They are trying, though not very hard, to comfort my mother, who in another era would be considered to be suffering from the vapors. Less tactful in the twenty-first century, I'd say she was losing it. That is, if I didn't know her better, know she was milking it for everything it was worth.

My mother loves attention. As it begins to flag, she swoons and claims to feel faint. Despite four No Smoking signs, my mother insists it's all right for her to light up because, after all, she's in shock. Not to mention that signs, as we know, don't apply to her.

When asked not to smoke, she collapses mournfully in a chair and lets her head loll to the side, all without mussing her hair.

Eventually, the detectives show up to find the four patrolmen all circled around her, debating whether to administer CPR, smelling salts or simply call the paramedics. I, however, know just what will snap her to attention.

"Detective Scoones," I say loudly. My mother parts the sea of cops.

"We have to stop meeting like this," he says lightly to me, but I can feel him checking me over with his eyes, making sure I'm all right while pretending not to care.

"What have you got in those pants?" my mother asks him, coming to her feet and staring at his crotch accusingly. "*Baydar?* Everywhere we Bayers are, you turn up. You don't expect me to buy that this is a co-incidence, I hope."

Drew tells my mother that it's nice to see her, too,

and asks if it's his fault that her daughter seems to attract disasters.

Charming to be made to feel like the bearer of a plague.

He asks how I am.

"Just peachy," I tell him. "I seem to be making a habit of finding dead bodies, my mother is driving me crazy and the catering hall I booked two freakin' years ago for Dana's bat mitzvah has just been shut down by the Board of Health!"

"Glad to see your luck's finally changing," he says, giving me a quick squeeze around the shoulders before turning his attention to the patrolmen, asking what they've got, whether they've taken any statements, moved anything, all the sort of stuff you see on TV, without any of the drama. That is, if you don't count my mother's threats to faint every few minutes when she senses no one's paying attention to her.

Mario tells his waitstaff to bring everyone espresso, which I decline because I'm wired enough. Drew pulls him aside and a minute later I'm handed a cup of coffee that smells divinely of Kahlúa.

The man knows me well. Too well.

His partner, whom I've met once or twice, says he'll

interview the kitchen staff. Drew asks Mario if he minds if he takes statements from the patrons first and gets to him and the waitstaff afterward.

"No, no," Mario tells him. "Do the patrons first." Drew raises his eyebrow at me like he wants to know if I get the double entendre. I try to look bored.

"What is it with you and murder victims?" he asks me when we sit down at a table in the corner.

I search them out so that I can see you again, I almost say, but I'm afraid it will sound desperate instead of sarcastic.

My mother, lighting up and daring him with a look to tell her not to, reminds him that *she* was the one to find the body.

Drew asks what happened *this time*. My mother tells him how the man in the john was "taken" with me, couldn't take his eyes off me and blatantly flirted with both of us. To his credit, Drew doesn't laugh, but his smirk is undeniable to the trained eye. And I've had my eye trained on him for nearly a year now.

"While he was noticing you," he asks me, "did *you* notice anything about him? Was he waiting for anyone? Watching for anything?"

I tell him that he didn't appear to be waiting or

watching. That he made no phone calls, was fairly intent on eating and did, indeed, flirt with my mother. This last bit Drew takes with a grain of salt, which was the way it was intended.

"And he had a short conversation with Mario," I tell him. "I think he might have been unhappy with the food, though he didn't send it back."

Drew asks what makes me think he was dissatisfied, and I tell him that the discussion seemed acrimonious and that Mario looked distressed when he left the table. Drew makes a note and says he'll look into it and asks about anyone else in the restaurant. Did I see anyone who didn't seem to belong, anyone who was watching the victim, anyone looking suspicious?

"Besides my mother?" I ask him, and Mom huffs and blows her cigarette smoke in my direction.

I tell him that there were several deliveries, the kitchen staff going in and out the back door to grab a smoke. He stops me and asks what I was doing checking out the back door of the restaurant.

Proudly—because, while he was off forgetting me, dropping by only once in a while to say hi to Jesse, my son, or drop something by for one of my daughters that he thought they might like, I was getting on with my life—I tell him that I'm decorating the place.

He looks genuinely impressed. "Commercial customers? That's great," he says. Okay, that's what he *ought* to say. What he actually says is "Whatever pays the bills."

"Howard Rosen, the famous restaurant critic, got her the job," my mother says. "You met him—the good-looking, distinguished gentleman with the *real* job, something to be proud of. I guess you've never read his reviews in *Newsday*."

Drew, without missing a beat, tells her that Howard's reviews are on the top of his list, as soon as he learns how to read.

"I only meant—" my mother starts, but both of us assure her that we know just what she meant.

"So," Drew says. "Deliveries?"

I tell him that Mario would know better than I, but that I saw vegetables come in, maybe fish and linens.

"This is the second restaurant job Howard's got her," my mother tells Drew.

"At least she's getting *something* out of the relationship," he says.

"If he were here," my mother says, ignoring the insinuation, "he'd be comforting her instead of interrogating her. He'd be making sure we're both all right after such an ordeal."

"I'm sure he would," Drew agrees, then looks me in the eyes as if he's measuring my tolerance for shock. Quietly he adds, "But then maybe he doesn't know just what strong stuff your daughter's made of."

It's the closest thing to a tender moment I can expect from Drew Scoones. My mother breaks the spell. "She gets that from me," she says.

Both Drew and I take a minute, probably to pray that's all I inherited from her.

"I'm just trying to save you some time and effort," my mother tells him. "My money's on Howard."

Drew withers her with a look and mutters something that sounds suspiciously like "fool's gold." Then he excuses himself to go back to work.

I catch his sleeve and ask if it's all right for us to leave. He says sure, he knows where we live. I say goodbye to Mario. I assure him that I will have some sketches for him in a few days, all the while hoping that this murder doesn't cancel his redecorating plans. I need the money desperately, the alternative being borrowing from my parents and being strangled by the strings.

My mother is strangely quiet all the way to her house. She doesn't tell me what a loser Drew Scoones is—despite his good looks—and how I was obviously drooling over him. She doesn't ask me where Howard is taking me tonight or warn me not to tell my father about what happened because he will worry about us both and no doubt insist we see our respective psychiatrists.

She fidgets nervously, opening and closing her purse over and over again.

"You okay?" I ask her. After all, she's just found a dead man on the toilet and tough as she is that's got to be upsetting.

When she doesn't answer me I pull over to the side of the road.

"Mom?" She refuses to meet my eyes. "You want me to take you to see Dr. Cohen?"

She looks out the window as if she's just realized we're on Broadway in Woodmere. "Aren't we near Marvin's Jewelers?" she asks, pulling something out of her purse.

"What have you got, Mother?" I ask, prying open her fingers to find the murdered man's ring.

"It was on the sink," she says in answer to my dropped jaw. "I was going to get his name and address and have you return it to him so that he could ask you out. I thought it was a sign that the two of you were meant to be together."

"He's dead, Mom. You understand that, right?" I ask. You never can tell when my mother is fine and when she's in la-la land.

"Well, I didn't know that," she shouts at me. "Not at the time."

I ask why she didn't give it to Drew, realize that she wouldn't give Drew the time in a clock shop and add, "…or one of the other policemen?"

"For heaven's sake," she tells me. "The man is dead, Teddi, and I took his ring. How would that look?"

Before I can tell her it looks just the way it is, she pulls out a cigarette and threatens to light it.

"I mean, really," she says, shaking her head like it's my brains that are loose. "What does he need with it now?"

By the Way, Did You Know You're Pregnant?

After twenty-five years of wedlock and three grown children, starting over with the diaper-and-formula scene was inconceivable for Laurel Mitchell. But between her tears and her husband's terror, they're waiting for a bundle of joy that's proving life's most unexpected gifts are the best.

The Second Time Around

by Marie Ferrarella

Available January 2007
TheNextNovel.com

HN73

HARLEQUIN
Next

All women become slightly psychic…eventually!

Lila's psychic ability disappeared
the moment her visions led her to
a missing heiress tied to the bed of
Lila's fiancé. Leaving town to start over,
Lila's journey finds her changing in
ways she could never have predicted.

Slightly Psychic

by Sandra Steffen

Available January 2007
TheNextNovel.com

HN75

HARLEQUIN®
Next™

Her daughter was
going through a Goth phase.

Her mother-in-law
was driving her crazy.

And something's up
with her husband.

Maybe she should dye her hair, lose those extra
pounds—anything to get the attention of the man
she loves. But what was he hiding? For the first
time in their marriage, they must be truly open
with each other to rediscover what brought them
together in the first place.

Sex, Lies and Cellulite: A Love Story

by Renee Roszel

REQUEST YOUR FREE BOOKS!

2 FREE NOVELS PLUS 2 FREE GIFTS!

There's the life you planned. And there's what comes next.

You can't give to others... until you give to yourself!

Supermom Abby Blake is going on strike. Having made her stand, Abby's not about to let anyone stop her—until her sworn enemy Cole whisks her away to Paris for some R & R. When the sparks start flying Abby thinks that maybe this "strike" should grow into a year-round holiday....

The Christmas Strike

by Nikki Rivers